SOUTH LANARKSHIRE
Leisure & Culture

www.library.southlanarkshire.gov.uk

South Lanarkshire Libraries

This book is to be returned on
or before the last date stamped
below or may be renewed by
telephone or online.

Delivering services for South Lanarkshire

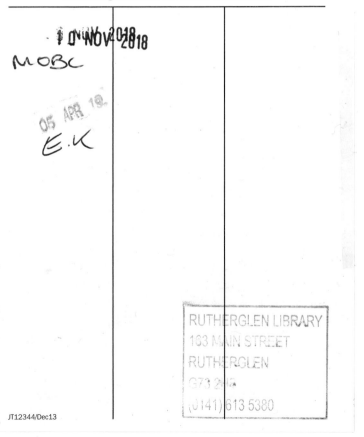
JT12344/Dec13

Gunsmoke over New Mexico

Nobody in the town of Tularosa is aware of the secret harboured by the proprietor of the local firearms store. The truth is that Sol Henshaw has never fired a gun in his life. All that changes when the infamous Clayburn Gang rob the bank in the sleepy New Mexico town.

Instinctively, Sol grabs the nearest revolver and runs into the street. A lucky shot kills the gang leader thus foiling the theft. Revered as a hero, Sol's picture is splashed across the front page of the Tularosa Tribune. The hot-headed younger brother of Rafe Clayburn also sees it and wants revenge.

But all does not go according to plan and innocent victims are placed in the firing line. How can Sol Henshaw save his family and bring the gang to justice? Much blood will be spilled before the final denouement.

Gunsmoke over New Mexico

Dale Graham

A Black Horse Western

ROBERT HALE · LONDON

© Dale Graham 2011
First published in Great Britain 2011

ISBN 978-0-7090-9242-1

Robert Hale Limited
Clerkenwell House
Clerkenwell Green
London EC1R 0HT

www.halebooks.com

Typeset by
Derek Doyle & Associates, Shaw Heath
Printed and bound in Great Britain by
CPI Antony Rowe, Chippenham and Eastbourne

ONE

HIDDEN AGENDA

Sol Henshaw was sweeping the veranda outside his gun shop in Tularosa. It was early morning and he had just opened up for the day. A warm sun was quickly burning off the mist cloaking the serrated peaks of the Sacramento Mountains to the east. It was going to be another hot one.

'Howdie, Mrs Lomax,' he called to a portly woman emerging from the dressmaker's next door. 'How's Hank doing?'

'Coming along just fine thanks, Sol,' replied the wife of the Flat Iron rancher who had recently broken his leg. Hank Lomax had been thrown by a wild bronc he was trying to bust. 'The stubborn old fool still thinks he's a young puncher and can do any job better than the regular hands. Now he's chafing at the bit to get back in the saddle.'

'You tell him from me to take it easy,' advised Sol. 'Ain't no sense in getting himself killed when he's got such a good family taking care of things. He should be enjoying the life he's built up over the years.'

'That's what I keep telling him,' muttered the concerned woman. 'But he don't take no notice.'

'Next time he's in town, I'll have a quiet word.' Sol tapped his nose guilefully, indicating that the advice would be firm and serious in its delivery. 'I'm sure he'll get the message.'

'That's mighty good of you, Sol,' replied Rachel Lomax whose round face took on a brighter composure. 'He'll listen to you.'

With that, the revitalized woman hurried off down the street.

A dreamy cast spread over the gun merchant's craggy façade. Life was idyllic in Tularosa. It was a sleepy town where nothing much happened. Sol often wondered how he managed to stay in business.

But the carrying of guns for personal protection was enshrined within the US Constitution, even if most folks never used them in anger. Save for the removal of vermin and the odd hunting trip, they somehow felt naked without one strapped to their hip.

The gun merchant had lived in Tularosa for a little over two years. During that time he had built up a thriving business.

In the West of 1877, virtually everybody carried a gun of some sort. Be it a tiny Deringer tucked into a lady's purse, or a Sharps Big Fifty capable of blasting a grizzly bear into the hereafter with a single shot.

But Sol Henshaw was one of the few citizens who avoided the conventional. And he harboured a secret.

In truth, Sol had never fired a gun in his life. Even though none of Tularosa's inhabitants had seen the merchant fire one of his own weapons, everybody automatically assumed he was a sharpshooter of the highest standard.

What purveyor of such armoury would not be?

Sol's acquisition of the business had come about by accident. His aversion to firearms stemmed from when he was a boy.

Jubal Henshaw's accidental shooting of his wife during a drunken spree had been witnessed by the youngster. The farmer had been cleaning a Spencer carbine when it had gone off. Sarah Henshaw had died instantly.

Sol had never forgiven his father. Soon after, he left the farm in Missouri and headed west. An amiable personality and a ready wit endeared him to all manner of folks thus enabling the young man to avoid trouble. In frontier settlements where guns were the normal means of settling arguments, Sol Henshaw chose to make good use of his hamlike fists.

Taking advantage of his skill in that department, he was able to make a steady living in the gloved version of bare-knuckle fighting called boxing. It was while engaged in this pursuit that he became acquainted with the daughter of his promoter.

The friendship soon blossomed into something

more intimate. However, the beautiful but strong-willed Maddy Robbins only agreed to a more amorous liaison if Battling Solomon King, as he was then known, would relinqush his brutal way of life in favour of a more mundane pursuit.

However, Maddy's father was loath to see his finest prospect abandon the boxing ring. The tough fighter was a good money-spinner. But Dandy Jim Robbins always put his daughter's wishes first. So it came about that the pair were married, the fight promoter appointing Sol as his business partner.

Some years later an official letter arrived informing Sol that he had been left a business in the town of Tularosa, New Mexico. An uncle on his mother's side had passed away and left it to the sole surviving relative. No details were given as to the type of business, only that it included a fully stocked emporium.

The inevitable conclusion reached was that it must be a general store. The Henshaws could not wait to take over.

Being one's own boss was the aspiration of most settlers on the Western frontier. Sol and Maddy Henshaw were no exception. And thus it came about that they said goodbye to the town of Broken Bow in Nebraska and headed south with their son Billy into a new life.

The realization of what they had inherited came as a hard shock to the system. But Sol was determined to make a go of it.

And he had no regrets. Life could not get any better than this.

*

At the same time as Sol Henshaw was musing over his good fortune, a gang of outlaws was awaiting their leader's return. The secret hideout was ensconced deep within the labyrinth of the Guadalupe Mountains.

The atmosphere inside the small cabin in Coyote Canyon crackled with suppressed tension. Three men were ranged around the main room, each wrapped in his own thoughts. One assiduously cleaned and oiled his revolver. Another whittled a hunk of timber with a lethal Bowie knife.

'D'yuh have to do that?' snapped the third and youngest of the trio. The constant chop chop of the blade was getting on his nerves.

Dominic Brewer, more generally known as Slippery Dom, gave the acerbic comment a lurid grin. His tongue flicked out across the razored edge of the glinting steel, lapping at the thin sliver of blood that appeared.

The kid's halting response to the macabre act drew a leery grin from the gunman. Brewer had acquired the odd nickname on account of his skeletal frame that, from an early age, had enabled him to enter houses through the narrowest of gaps.

And so began a life of crime.

'You gettin' nervous, kid?' He smirked.

Eddie Clayburn threw a caustic glower towards the speaker. Even though he was a good ten years younger than Brewer, he still hated being regarded as a greenhorn. And because the missing fourth member and leader of the outlaw gang was his brother, the young hardcase figured more respect was due. His hand flew to the gun on his hip.

Brewer laughed. 'My mistake . . . Eddie,' he said, raising a placatory hand. 'Why don't yuh just take it easy. Rafe'll be back soon enough.'

The older man just couldn't resist baiting the feisty kid. He scratched a vesta on his faded jeans and applied the flaring match to a cigar. Then he continued with the whittling. Eddie Clayburn lurched to his feet, gave Brewer another mordant scowl and headed for the door of the cabin.

'I need some air.' He sniffed with meaningful intent. 'This dump is startin' to reek some'n awful.' The implication was aimed at Brewer's less than fragrant personal aroma.

Dom snarled out a lurid curse and raised the knife to launch it at the kid's strutting figure. He had no intention of killing Eddie, just scaring him a little. And maybe drawing a little of the red stuff.

'Cut the wranglin', you knuckleheads!' The blunt reproof came from the third outlaw. Otero grabbed the hovering arm and forced it down. He was a stocky dude boasting a compact frame that was all hard muscle. 'Save it for whatever the boss has in mind on this next caper.'

He and Rafe Clayburn had been together since the war. They had run with the notorious Bloody Bill Anderson. Robbing and killing in the name of the Confederate cause had proved to be both exhilarating and highly lucrative. It was also considered legitimate action by the powers that be. Once the war had finished, many of the guerrilla bands found life dull in comparison.

The two buddies joined up with the renowned James Gang for a spell before going their own way. Ten years later and they were still at large. This had been primarily due to their sticking with smaller jobs where protection of the haul was not considered a priority by the authorities.

It also meant, however, that the profits were equally sparse.

No matter how close the pair had grown over the years, Otero knew that he could never compete where blood kin was concerned. Rafe Clayburn would protect his headstrong brother to the death if needs be. And the gang boss had a habit of keeping future plans under wraps. Sometimes it rankled. But Otero had learned to accept it.

For some time now he had been pushing his buddy to go for more rewarding jobs. Rafe had been less enthusiastic, preferring to stick with a more cautious approach. The simmering disagreement had finally come to a head the previous month when their latest heist had gone badly wrong.

That had been a close shave and no mistake. They were lucky to have escaped with only one casualty. The tough outlaw cast his mind back, the whole sorry episode tumbling into sharp focus.

The Clayburn Gang were heading towards Cochise Pass at a fast canter, a dustcloud following in their wake.

'Why are we in such an all-fired hurry, Rafe?' queried the boss's younger brother. 'And when you gonna spill the beans about this job you been plannin' for the last month?'

Rafe Clayburn emitted a sigh of frustration. Much as he felt responsible for his younger kin, the rugged outlaw often wanted to clamp a muzzle to the kid's overactive mouth. He put it down to youthful exuberance.

'You know darned well that I never divulge any details until the last minute just to keep things nice and tight,' he hawked back with vigour. 'Some rannies in this outfit have a bad habit of warblin' off at the mouth after a few drinks.' A reproachful eye was fastened on to his brother. 'Do I have to remind you about what happened last fall?'

Eddie's cheeks reddened. He detested any recall of the incident.

On that occasion, an overindulgence of hard liquor supplied by a wily drifter had loosened the kid's tongue. Unknowingly, he had revealed the details of a forthcoming stage robbery. The ever-watchful Otero had become suspicious when the critter had abruptly left the Artesia saloon.

Following close on the varmint's heels, he observed him heading straight for the local tinstar's office. Otero peered through the grimy window to witness a seedy powwow unfolding. And it was obvious that it involved the negotiation of a cut of the reward money when the gang were captured, or killed. Otero was well aware that he alone was worth

$500 – Dead or Alive!

The simmering outlaw mouthed a silent curse. He waited for the the slimy rat to leave the office and ride off in the direction of Alamogordo. Once he had figured out the guy's probable destination, Otero took a back trail that brought him out ahead of the double-dealer.

A single shot from his Springfield ensured that the bastard would not be collecting his blood money.

Back at the cabin beside Coyote Creek, Otero had apprised the gang leader of the problem. As a result, the robbery had been brought forward a week. Caught unawares, the stageline had opted for an old driver close to retirement and no guard. Cynics might claim they did it to save money, thinking that the week's payroll was safe.

It was a walkover, easier than falling off a log. The incident became a standing joke amongst the gang after Rafe sent a sarcastic wire to the Artesia lawdog. In it, he expressed the hope that the sheriff had not been inconvenienced too much when the gang failed to turn up at the expected rendezvous.

Eddie's part in the shady affair was not overlooked. And Rafe's displeasure was not confined to harsh words. It had taken a month for the bruises both to the kid's body and to his self-esteem to disappear. But the beating had resulted in the desired effect.

Eddie Clayburn had learned to keep his mouth buttoned. But Rafe was taking no further chances.

So here they were, sheltering in the shade of a

soaring overhang. There were two hours to spare before the wagon carrying the monthly bank deposit was due. Time enough to apprise the boys of the situation and the manner in which he wanted it played out.

'How did you learn about this delivery to the bank's head office at Hobbs?' enquired Dom Brewer of the gang boss.

Clayburn offered the speaker a wry smirk. He lit a quirley before evincing a reply.

'Eddie here learned his lesson the hard way.' He chuckled.

The gang members gave their young confederate a series of knowing leers. The younger Clayburn snarled back an indeterminate grunt, his smoothly youthful cheeks perceptibly reddening. It would take a month of Sundays for him to live down his indiscretion.

'But others ain't got a considerate brother to show them the error of their ways.' Rafe slapped his squirming kin on the back. Laughs all round. 'A certain bank teller also found his mouth galloping off after I'd plied him with a few drinks last time I was in Carlsbad. He told me that the bank had found it safer to take the lesser known trail through the Guadalupe Mountains by way of Cochise Pass.'

'How much do we have to pay him for this information?' interjected the wary voice of Otero.

'Not a goddamed thing,' replied a breezy Rafe Clayburn. 'That's the beauty of the scheme. The poor jasper was so darned drunk that I had to carry him back to his lodging house. There's no chance that he could recall anything that was discussed.'

'Let's hope not,' mused Otero pensively.

Clayburn shrugged off his buddy's over-cautious remark. 'You worry too much, Otero.' Then to the others, 'OK, boys. Let's get into position.'

On each side of the trail, tall yellow-flowered yucca stems swayed in the gentle breeze like a troupe of dancing girls. Overhead, a flight of cactus wrens flew past, unaware that the tranquil scene was about to be torn asunder.

Five minutes later the steady pounding of shod hoofs assailed their senses as the wagon hove into view. Rafe's eagle eye noted that there was only a driver aboard together with the guard riding shotgun.

Emerging from the cover afforded by a cluster of boulders, he snapped a couple of shots into the air. The others ranged on either side of the wagon, guns drawn and ready for use if necessary.

'Hoist 'em high, boys!' hollered the gang leader. 'Toss them hoglegs down and don't make no false moves.'

With barely a flicker, the two men ditched their weapons and raised their arms skyward.

Rafe frowned. Something didn't quite fit. These dudes were acting too cool. Not the slightest hint of resistance. And their faces hadn't even registered any surprise at this unexpected heist. It was as if they were expecting something to happen.

He cast a quick look around. That was when he

noticed a glint of sunlight on metal over in the rocks on the far side of the pass.

His eyes widened perceptibly.

A trap! They had walked into a goldarned set-up!

That teller must have realized what he'd let slip. No doubt the critter had concocted some tale to save his neck as to how he heard the plan being discussed. And now he could legitimately claim a reward for checkmating the robbery. All this flashed through Rafe's active brain in a split second.

'Back off, boys,' he yelled, firing haphazardly towards the rocks where the hidden ambushers were now emerging. 'It's a trap. We've been fooled. Let's get outa here, pronto!'

That was when all hell broke loose.

Gunfire erupted from at least a dozen weapons. The gang dug spurs into their frightened mounts. Keeping low while hugging their necks, they took flight. Bullets pinged and zipped all around, richocheting and whining off the rocks. A cry to his rear told Rafe that one of his men had been hit. But he was accorded no time to think who that might be with hot lead plucking at his sleeve.

Luckily, the rising dustcloud helped to conceal the gang's escape.

Only when he felt certain they had given the pursuing posse the slip did Rafe call a halt to rest the horses. That was when he discovered they were one man down.

'Chase didn't make it, boss.' Slippery Dom Brewer's remark was subdued. He and the Colorado owlhoot had been close buddies. Chase Daggert might have been a touch slow in the brain department but he made up for it with a lethal gunhand plus a winning smile for the ladies. On this occasion, unfortunately, he had paid the ultimate penalty for his lethargic reaction to the boss's verbal warning.

Rafe was seething. Normally cool as a mountain stream, none of the others had seen him so riled up. His heavily contoured face had assumed the colour of a setting sun. Narrowing eyes burned just as fiercely. And it was towards himself that his anger was aimed. He had lost face on account of this fiasco. And it hurt.

Such a situation could not go unresolved. He would have to rectify the error. And quickly!

'You boys head back to the cabin,' he rasped, injecting as much vehemence into the order as he could muster. 'I got things to do.'

'Where yuh goin', Rafe?'

The gang boss shot his brother a look of pure venom.

'Nobody makes a monkey out of Rafe Clayburn.' He mouthed the words in a sibilant growl. 'That teller has made his last payout.' And with that threat, he spurred off in the direction of Carlsbad.

TWO

A NEW RECRUIT

Eddie Clayburn was getting restive as he stamped back into the cabin. It had been five days since Rafe had lit out for Carlsbad.

'How long does it take to give some bank johnny a belly full of lead?' he mouthed to anyone who would listen, but not expecting a response from the lounging gunnies.

He got one anyway, from Otero.

'He's probably made a detour back through Tularosa to suss out that bank. Make certain there ain't no drawbacks.'

'Has Rafe given you any idea about this Tularosa job?' Brewer enquired, addressing his query to the skittish younger Clayburn. Blowing out a perfect smoke ring, Brewer eyed the youngster from beneath thick beetled brows. 'Seeing as how he allus takes you into his confidence.' Slippery Dom could see the kid visibly rising to the bait. He just couldn't resist the challenge.

But experience had taught him that humouring Eddie Clayburn by seeking his opinion always served to sweeten the boy's quick temper. 'It's just that I allus look on you as the son I never had.'

The comment was laced heavily with sarcastic undertones that were, however, lost on the kid. It served to mollify the fiery redhead. Eddie relaxed his lean-limbed frame while considering the enquiry posed by his confederate.

He shrugged.

'Rafe did hint that the bank in Tularosa acts as a clearing house for all the ranchers in the territory.'

'So there oughta be a hefty wad of dough just a-waitin' for some enterprisin' guys like us to remove.' observed the thoughtful Brewer, resuming his carving of an Indian totem.

'You got it in one, Slip.' Eddie smirked while flipping the cork from a bottle of whiskey. He poured a generous three-fingered measure into a glass and downed the liquor in a single gulp. 'Once this haul's in the bag, we can all head down to El Paso for some relaxation over the winter.'

'Now that's some'n we all deserve,' commented Brewer.

Otero was about to warn the kid to go easy on the hard stuff when a pounding of hoofs outside the cabin brought all three hardcases to their feet.

Guns palmed, they moved across to the window.

'Its Rafe!' Eddie Clayburn bustled out on to the

veranda. Then his eyes widened. 'And he's got some dude with him.'

The other two quickly joined him.

'Where in thunderation have you been?' Eddie snapped before the gang boss had time to dismount. 'We've all been chewin' leather in this dump.' Before his brother could respond, Eddie snapped, 'And who's this jasper?'

Rafe ignored the question.

The others moved aside as he entered the cabin in company with the stranger who displayed the stealthy demeanour of a deadly predator. His right hand hovered above a cross-draw holster. Beady eyes flickered. Black, and cold as ice, they challenged anyone to disapprove of his unexpected advent.

'Give me a drink!' demanded Rafe. 'My throat's drier than a temperance hall.' Otero pushed across the half-empty bottle that Eddie had been nursing. Nobody spoke. Rafe Clayburn would make the introductions in his own good time.

After taking a generous slurp, he handed the bottle to his companion.

'This is Cropper John Beswick,' he said. 'He's takin' over from Chase.'

The newcomer slowly lifted the bottle to his fleshy lips while carefully appraising each of the outlaws in turn. Still he didn't speak.

'Anybody got any problems with that?' This time it was Rafe whose steady gaze panned the room.

Like curious children, their eyes were drawn to the ragged lump of blackened flesh attached to the left

side of Cropper John's head. The brutal disfigure-
ment spoilt what would otherwise have been a
handsome visage. It had originally earned him the
moniker of Crop-eared John, which had been
quickly shortened to Cropper.

The gouged earlobe quivered as Beswick dispelled
their unspoken nosiness.

'And before them peepers bust out of your heads,'
the guy's voice was a deep baritone, scratchy and
harsh as if his throat was being twisted; the words
emerging as a menacing growl, 'I got this from a
sneakin' rat of a gambler who'd falsely accused me of
palming cards.'

The threatening glower offered a challenge to
anyone whose mug even hinted of a smile. Nobody
chose to accept the proferred gauntlet.

'And if'n I ever come across that lyin' bastard
again, my own knife will be put to good use.' John
whipped out a double-edged blade and slammed it
into the table.

Nobody spoke.

Eventually Otero broke the tense atmosphere.

'How'd you two meet?'

Rafe considered the question before replying. But
it was Beswick who supplied the answer.

'I rode with Quantrill during the war,' rasped the
newcomer, relaxing now as the rest of the gang
averted their gaze from the mangled appendage.
'After the Lawrence raid the gang split. We intended
joining up again before heading south for Texas.
Unfortunately, I was caught and strung up by a stray

patrol of blue-bellies.' Beswick fingered the livid scar encircling his neck. He glanced across at the gang leader. 'Lucky for me old Rafe here just happened along at the right time, else I'd have been strummin' a harp.'

'More likely stokin' up the fires of hell,' chuckled Rafe.

They both laughed at the facetious comment, although John's response was more akin to a rabid snarl. The joke appeared to release the tension in the cabin as Rafe continued with the tale.

'We met up again just by chance in a saloon while I was checking out the lie of the land in Tularosa.'

'Times change, people change,' Cropper John interjected. 'Its been twelve years since our trails last crossed. But a guy never forgets the dude what saved his bacon.' There was respect, even a measure of awe, in the way he looked at the gang boss. 'When he told me what you boys were plannin' and how you were a man down, I just had to offer my services.'

'And John here is no mean hand with that Remington he's totin',' added Rafe injecting an equal measure of regard into the assertion. 'Show the boys what you can do, Cropper.'

The new recruit peered around the room, eyeing up a suitable target. His narrow gaze lit upon an ace of spades pinned to the back wall. In the time it takes to draw breath, his hand was filled. An ear-shattering blast pounded the thick walls of the cabin as John emptied his revolver. When the smoke had dispersed, all eyes focused on the playing card.

Eddie Clayburn snorted.

'That ain't so good,' he sneered. 'A baby could do better. There's only one hole in the card.'

'Take a closer look, kid,' hissed his brother, a tight smile drawing the thin lips apart. Eddie stood up and swaggered over to the pinioned card. Removing it he stuck a finger through the ragged hole in the black spot. 'Now look at the wall behind,' Rafe snapped.

The others had now joined him. It was Slippery Dom who made the mind-boggling discovery.

'Six bullets, one hole.' A whistle of amazement issued from between pursed lips. 'Man! That surely is the best shootin' I ever did see.' He fastened a twisted grin on to a stunned Eddie Clayburn. 'Wouldn't you say so, kid?'

Eddie responded with a noncommital shrug, though it was clear that the gunman's prowess had struck home. The flinty look in his eye, however, indicated that one day the two of them would have to find out who was the faster draw.

The ever pragmatic Otero brought the conversation round to the main purpose of Rafe Clayburn's recent absence.

'Did you settle with that Judas bank teller, Rafe?'

Clayburn replied with a surly grunt, his narrowed gaze assuming a cold intensity.

'I waited until the critter had finished work at the bank and was heading back to his house on the north side of Carlsbad,' he said taking another swig from the whiskey bottle. 'After buffaloing the bastard, I strung him up to the nearest tree by his feet.' Rafe chuckled at the recollection.

'I bet he didn't cotton to that, eh Rafe?' urged his animated brother eager for more details.

'Too right,' breezed the gang boss. 'The guy was crapping himself. It smelt some'n awful.' He wrinkled his nose. The others laughed. 'Then I let him have it with both barrels of the Loomis. There weren't much left to recognize after that.'

'Anybody see yuh?' queried the ever-careful Otero.

Rafe scoffed. 'Take me for some kinda greenhorn? Anyway, it was dark by that time so it was simple just to vanish into the night before any snoopers came to investigate.'

He paused to roll a quirley.

'But I left a message pinned to the body. And it read . . .' The gang hung on his every word, mouths agape. Rafe was enjoying himself. A wistful smile played dreamily across the rugged contours of his face as he blew out a plume of blue smoke before finishing. *This is what happens to skunks that mess with the Clayburns*!

'You reckon we'll be more famous than the James Gang after this, Rafe?' prompted Eddie, slapping his thigh. He was more than eager to acquire a notorious reputation as a feared owlhoot.

'Robbing the bank in Tularosa should seal it, little brother,' Rafe answered him. The warped grin displayed a set of tobacco-stained choppers.

'So this job is definitely on then?' pressed Otero.

'Sure is, boys.' The gang leader smiled. 'And Friday is when we'll pull it. The bank will be chock-full of readies after the ranchers make their monthly deposits.'

'That gives us four days,' mused a thoughtful Dom Brewer.

'This guy is one sharp cookie,' rasped Cropper hoarsely. Apart from Brewer, who received the light-hearted dig with an aggrieved frown, the others laughed uproariously. Beswick had clearly been fully accepted into the gang. The ugly mark was all but forgotten.

'Right in one,' agreed Rafe joining in the hilarity. 'So we ain't got a moment to lose. He pushed back his chair and stood up. Draining the coffee mug was a signal for the others also to make a move. 'Get your gear together and be ready to ride in an hour,' he ordered.

THREE

HARSH WORDS

Rafe Clayburn raised his hand, calling a halt on the outskirts of Tularosa. Narrowing eyes panned the huddle of buildings that comprised the small town. It looked no different from a hundred others the gang had passed through during their long and varied career on the wrong side of the law.

Clapboard structures lined the wide main thoroughfare. Most were single-storey affairs apart from the hotel, which also boasted an upper veranda. Squared-off false fronts made them appear larger and more imposing than they were in reality. Apart from the brick-built bank, all were constructed of pitch pine. Behind and arrayed in a more haphazard manner were to be seen an assortment of individual dwellings and corrals.

Tularosa's prosperity was overtly displayed in the form of oil-burning streetlights. The town council

26

even employed a man to maintain them.

'Looks a bit of a one-horse town to me,' opined Eddie with a disdainful sniff.

'Maybe that's cos you ain't done the plannin',' snapped his brother.

'Swinburn's Bank handles all the receipts from surrounding ranches,' interposed Cropper John. The gunman had been making his own discreet enquiries prior to meeting up with Rafe Clayburn. 'And if'n you open yer eyes, kid, you'll see that this is mighty fine country for raisin' prime beef.'

Eddie Clayburn snarled. He didn't cotton to this new rannie treating him like a puddleheaded halfwit. His clenched fists rose theateningly.

Rafe instantly picked up on the fractious tension.

'Save the bickerin' for when this job is in the bag,' he rapped, arrowing a caustic frown at his new recruit. The order for both men to pocket their differences was punched out with vigour. The gang boss had no intention of having this caper jeopardized by petty wrangles.

'The bank is halfway down on the right. We'll meet up outside,' he declared firmly. Then, leaning on his saddle horn, Rafe eyed each man in turn. 'And take it nice and easy when you ride in. No sharp movements. That way nobody will suspect anythin'.' His next remark was aimed at Slippery Dom. 'You hold the horses as usual.'

'Sure thing, boss.'

'Anybody see a problem with this?' Nobody spoke. 'So you all know what has to be done?' Curt nods all round. Now that the die was cast, a tense atmosphere had gripped the gang. 'Then let's ride.'

Rafe took the lead, nudging his horse forward.

It was another hot Friday afternoon in Tularosa.

Folks were going about their normal business. Leaning on his broomhandle in a pensive mood, Sol Henshaw's thoughts had strayed from the job in hand. Lines of worry creased his forehead. His eight-year-old son Billy had been giving the guns displayed in the store more than just a passing glance. Sooner rather than later, the boy was going to start asking questions that Sol was loath to answer.

So intent was he on his own problems that he failed to heed the arrival in town of the five strangers. Perhaps that was because Rafe Clayburn had insisted the gang entered Tularosa separately to avoid arousing undue curiosity.

'Hey, Sol!' A gruff voice roughened by too much hard liquor called out from inside the shop. 'Any chance of you rustling up that coffee what was promised a half-hour ago?'

The summons jerked the gun merchant from his wistful reverie. He hustled back inside the shop. Mort Allerdyce, the local tinstar, and Doc Farthing were engaged in their regular game of chess. The pair of aging reprobates often met in the gunshop to chew the breeze over a game and a few cups of fresh Arbuckles.

'I'll get Maddy to hurry up, fellas,' Sol assured his visitors.

Although the best of friends, the duo could never stop arguing. If it wasn't the weather and the price of beef, it was the fees charged by the medic, or the guilt or otherwise of the latest incumbent of the hoosegow.

Sol couldn't help smiling as the banter continued.

The arrival of the coffee instantly stilled the palaver. Both of the older men were transfixed as always.

Maddy Henshaw was definitely worth more than a passing glance. A willowy blonde, tall and statuesque; Sol never stopped thanking his lucky stars that such a delectable creature had chosen him over innumerable other suitors who had courted her in the past.

What could she have possibly seen in a scarred and bruised knuckleduster like him? They were like chalk and cheese to look at, but loved each other more than life itself.

'Ain't you scallawags got no manners?' hooted Sol with a tongue-in-cheek glance towards his beautiful wife. Maddy assumed a serious mien as she placed the steaming cups before her guests.

'S-sorry about that, Maddy,' the marshal blurted out. 'It's just that. . . .'

'What my jackass of a friend is trying to say,' simpered the preening medic, taking a sip of the delicious brew, 'is that being a confirmed bachelor has . . . now how should I put it. . . ?' Doc Farthing made a deliberate pause, tapping his chin in thought. 'Well, it's tended to blunt his etiquette where the opposite sex is concerned.'

Allerdyce blustered some, puffing out his ruddy cheeks and throwing a piercing look of disapproval at his colleague. 'That ain't so,' he railed. 'Maisy Tibbs has never complained about my darned . . . etiquette!!' Then a crafty smile flashed across the wizened visage. A rapid hand-movement followed as the black knight on the game board was followed by a howl of triumph. 'So beat that if'n you can, clever clogs. Checkmate!'

The doctor's mouth opened in surprise, his neat moustache quivering at his having been outwitted.

'Ugh!' ejaculated the startled loser. 'That weren't fair. You distracted my concentration.'

Allerdyce shook his head, chuckling gleefully at his partner's discomfiture. Slapping his thighs, he galloped on with a concluding declaration.

'So that makes it your turn to pay for dinner tonight, Mister Sawbones.'

Maddy Henshaw stood watching the two old buddies, a bemused look on her aquiline features. 'When are you pair of old buzzards going to get along without this big hoohaa every day?'

'You know darn well that ain't never gonna happen,' averred Sol firmly, his rugged features sporting a broad grin.

At that moment the door of the shop opened and three boys rushed in.

'Hey, Pa!' gasped the smallest of the trio, tripping over his boots and sprawling on to the wooden floor.

'Whoa there, Billy,' admonished Sol, picking his son up and dusting off his trousers. 'Why are you jaspers in such an all-fired hurry?'

'Chuck's pa is gonna teach him how to fire a gun.' The little guy slung a thumb at one his larger buddies. 'When you gonna teach me, Pa?'

Then, without any thought to the consequences, young Billy reached for a shiny new Colt Peacemaker on the counter.

Sol's reaction was immediate. His face clouded over, a red flush blossoming across the twitching face.

'How many times do I have to say it,' he shouted grabbing the gun and pushing his son away. 'Keep your hands off these darned things. They're much too dangerous for a young kid. Only them what understands the danger involved should handle them.'

The angry outburst was totally at odds with Sol's normally placid character. And he instantly regretted it. A brief glance at the others gathered around told him they were equally stunned by the merchant's unexpected tirade.

Sol's deepest fear had materialized. And he had been caught unawares, giving a panicky, knee-jerk reaction.

Surrounded by firearms, it was inevitable that his son would some day want to be like all the others. But to Sol's way of thinking, strapping on a gunbelt was like shaving. You only did it when you were old enough. And an eight-year-old kid sure wasn't that.

Now it had been brought out into the open. Sol sucked in a deep breath, glanced at his anxious wife, then back at the pleading eyes of the young boy. He quickly attempted to defuse the tense situation.

'All in good time, Billy,' he announced, ruffling the boy's hair while trying to keep the tremulous quiver in his throat under control.

'But Pa—'

'No buts!' Sol barked rather too snappily, wagging a pointed finger. 'You ain't old enough to be handling deadly weapons yet. Chuck and Tom here are bigger and older than you. And they live on ranches.' A yearning hope still lingered in the boy's eyes. But Sol was unmoved. 'Now that's an end to it.'

Observing that his plea had fallen on stony ground, Billy Henshaw's head drooped on to his narrow chest. Not wanting to crush his son's spirit, Sol dug his fist into a jar of candy sticks on the counter. He also wanted to divert attention away from the original purpose of the visit.

'Everything comes to him who waits,' he observed with a tentative smile as he handed out the colourful treats. 'And don't say I never give you anything.'

The faces of all three youngsters brightened. Candy was usually reserved for special occasions.

'Gee thanks, Mr Henshaw,' enthused Chuck Bradley, grabbing the candy and poking it into his mouth before it could be removed.

The original reason for visiting the gun shop was indeed forgotten as the three friends hustled out on to the street. Slurping noises followed the closing of the door.

Sol was relieved that the prickly incident had been

forgotten. A sigh of relief escaped from between tight lips. But he was under no illusions that it would resurface again at some point in the none too distant future. He was seriously going to have to decide how best to tackle the odious dilemma.

It happened far sooner than anticipated as Mort Allerdyce put him well and truly on the spot.

'You can't keep the boy wrapped in cotton wool for ever, Sol,' he remarked. 'In this part of the country he needs to be able to handle himself. And that means toting a hogleg.'

'Every argument don't always have to be settled with a blazing Colt,' rapped the doc. 'That's *your* answer to everything.'

FOUR

HOLD UP!

Rafe Clayburn kept his hat pulled low, more to hide his face than shade out the late afternoon sun. The gang boss always chose this time of day when a bank job was to be pulled. Arriving just before the doors were closed ensured they would not be disturbed. Friday was always preferred because that was when the vaults held the most dough.

Nobody took any heed of the dust-caked rider ambling down the street. Just another drifter looking for work on one of the many ranches to the east. Rafe glanced down a narrow alley and gave a terse nod of approval at what caught his eye. West of Tularosa lay a bleak expanse of white sand that offered the perfect escape route over which to disappear into the San Andreas Mountains.

He drew his mount to a halt some fifty yards beyond the bank and tied up to a hitching rail.

Dismounting, he casually lit a quirly, and waited. Eagle eyes panned the street searching for any sign that he was under observation. Nothing out of the ordinary disturbed the placid calm.

One by one the other members of the gang saun-tered into town. Each dismounted at a different spot. A nod from Rafe and they began casually walking their horses down towards the bank.

Hand resting on the door handle, Rafe paused. He cast a final look around to ensure no curious stares were directed their way. Then, quick as a flash, he shouldered through the doors into the cool inte-rior of Swinburn's Bank. Luckily there were no late customers to deal with.

The gang boss drew his revolver and shouted, 'Don't nobody move. This is a stick-up. Co-operate and you go home in one piece. Now open that vault and fill these bags.'

John Beswick threw a couple of white flour sacks over the counter. So stunned were the bank's employees that nobody moved or uttered a word. It was Eddie Clayburn who broke the spell that gripped the ogling tellers.

'You heard the man,' he hollered. 'Now shift yer asses *rapido*, or get drilled where yuh stand. We ain't playin' games here.'

'S-sure, mister,' stuttered a grey-haired veteran who was due for retirement and had every intention of collecting his pension. The old dude quickly began shovelling change from his counter drawer into a bag. Eddie nervously waved his gun to encourage the oldster.

'D-don't shoot,' croaked the cashier. 'I'm going as fast as I can.'

'Leave that small stuff,' Rafe snapped. 'Notes only.'

That was when the bank manager emerged from his office, having been disturbed by the noisy outburst.

'What's all the racket out here?' he piped up in a reedy voice.

His mouth dropped open when he saw the four masked men with drawn guns. A small, rather insignificant-looking jasper with a bald pate and pompous manner, Hyram Swinburn boasted a waxed moustache. Intended to present a more regal image, it actually made him look more like a strutting gnome.

However, the guy was no milksop. Swinburn had not risen to become a respected and able bank manager without the possession of a subtle and agile brain. Unphased by the stark reality of being confronted by a gang of hard-boiled desperadoes, he quickly interposed.

'The vault is on a time lock and can't be opened until tomorrow morning. So you're wasting your time. All we have in here is small change.'

As it happened, he had not yet set the timer, but assumed these varmints would not cotton on to that fact. Unfortunately he hadn't bargained with the astute 'financial' experience of Rafe Clayburn in these matters.

'You're lyin', mister,' snarled the irate robber. 'I know darn well that vault ain't set until you leave the bank. Now open it double quick or I'll ventilate your mangy hide.' He jabbed the snout of the lethal shooter into the little man's ear.

All eyes were now focused on the sweating bank boss, who slowly reached into his pocket for the key.

All, that was except for Jarvis Hall. The head cashier now saw his chance to turn the tables on these desperadoes. His hand slid towards a lower drawer where he kept a six-gun for just such an emergency. The gun lifted and swung towards the elder Clayburn.

But Cropper John had witnessed the sly manoeuvre. His own pistol whipped round. Fanning the hammer, he pumped a half-load into the overzealous clerk. Blood fountained from the three puncture wounds. Hall slid out of sight behind the counter.

'That's torn it!' called out the anxious voice of Otero as he backed towards the door. 'I'll keep a lookout while you clear the vault, Rafe.'

The gang boss nodded. He swung his hogleg down across the bank manager's head as anger at this setback to their plans bit deep. Swinburn slumped over a filing cabinet, blood dribbling from a lacerated scalp wound.

Outside a dog barked. Others had likely also heard the shots and would be coming to investigate.

'Hurry it up, Rafe,' shouted a twitchy Eddie Clayburn, 'and let's get outa here, pronto.'

'Not before I get what we came for,' snarled the gang boss, who was not about to be rushed.

Panicking at this stage in the heist would only make things worse. After rifling through the manager's pockets, he grabbed the keys and opened up the vault. A lurid grin split the rugged features as he beheld the wads of banknotes. Hurriedly he filled a sack, then tossed it over the counter to Beswick. 'Here, John,' he snapped. 'You take charge of this while I fill the other one.'

'Don't be too long, Rafe,' hissed Otero, whose stoic demeanour was beginning to crack. 'Folks are looking over here. We should be leavin' now.'

Rafe growled out a vivid epithet, but recognized that his sidekick was right. 'OK, let's go!' he yelled, making a dash for the door.

Brewer had the horses ready. Each man leapt into his saddle and galloped off up the street in the opposite direction from which they had entered the town.

Inside Henshaw's gun shop the usual contrary wrangling would have continued as usual had not the discourse been interrupted by a sudden flurry of sharp reports from outside. Eight pairs of bulging orbs swivelled towards the window.

The unmistakable crackle of gunfire saw all four scrambling to their feet.

'The bank's been robbed!'

The strident announcement from outside the store was immediately followed by another flurry of shots. But it was his son's panic-stricken yell that found Sol reaching for the Colt revolver that so recently had caused his uncharacteristic aggravation.

It was an instinctive move. His kin was in danger.

'Leave it!' The gritty command came from Mort Allerdyce. No longer the whirlwind of law and order he had once been, the marshal still had steel in his backbone. Sol's hand faltered above the ivory butt. 'This is where I earn that salary the council pays me every month.'

The lawdog hustled across to the open door, his six-gun palmed and fully cocked. Surprisingly nimble-footed for an old dude, a purposeful glint twinkled in his eye. It had been a long time since unwarranted gunplay had sought his attention.

He rushed outside, planting his stocky frame in the middle of the street just as the robbers were making good their escape. Sol was more concerned for the safety of his son. Luckily, Billy Henshaw had only been scared by the flying lead that was intended to keep heads down. It had worked. Billy was splayed flat out on the boardwalk alongside his frightened buddies.

Sol quickly chivvied them inside the shop.

'In the name of the law, I order you to—' Allerdyce had unpinned his badge and was holding it aloft. But that was as far as he got. Two bullets punched him back as the escaping bank robbers thundered past. Hoots of derision greeted the unheeded summons to surrender.

The lawman's body twisted with the harsh impact, spinning round like a child's top. He was dead before his body hit the ground.

But another citizen of Tularosa was more fortunate.

Russ Bradley had been wandering down the street to pick up his son Chuck when the shooting started. Like most other folks in the sleepy town he had been stunned into immobility by the sudden and violent events that had so rapidly unfolded. But Russ was a doughty Texan. He shrugged off the lethargic stupor on realizing that his life savings were about to disappear.

He dashed over to his horse, snatched the old Henry carbine from its saddle boot and jammed the rifle into his shoulder.

Lever and fire! Lever and fire!

Two deep-thoated roars pursued the felons up the street. The first clipped the sign fronting Sol Henshaw's gun shop. But the second ploughed into the back leg of Rafe Clayburn's horse. The stricken animal stumbled, throwing its rider into the dust, then keeled over in a welter of thrashing hoofs.

The gang leader was unhurt and leapt to his feet, reaching for his own rifle. Down the street aways, Bradley's eyes widened. Seeing that his aim had been less than accurate, he took a more careful bead on the horseless robber.

Lever and . . . click! Nothing. He tried again; still nothing. Then he remembered. Numerous rounds had already been used on the way into town when he and Chuck had been potting varmints. The farmer cursed, wishing he'd had the good sense to reload.

Too late now. The outlaw threw a malevolent grimace towards his prey as his own long gun rose.

But it was never fired.

Sol Henshaw was standing in the street, a smoking Colt .45 gripped in his right hand. Rafe Clayburn's mouth dropped open in surprise. Staggering back, he tumbled over his dying horse, and never got up. Sol just stood there, dumbfounded, unable to comprehended the gravity of his actions. His own mouth likewise hung ajar as he stared at the outlaw's splayed form.

Meanwhile the other outlaws had paused at the edge of town. On realizing that his brother had been shot, Eddie swung his own mount around. His intention was to go back and help his fallen brother and retrieve the loot. Otero had other ideas. The veteran outlaw grabbed the kid's reins.

'He's dead, Eddie,' he rapped harshly. 'There ain't nothin' any of us can do for him now.'

But Eddie was past caring. 'Let go, damn it!' he yelled, tears forming in his eyes. 'I gotta help him.'

He tried to wrench free of the iron grip. But on the other side Brewer grasped the bridle. 'He's right, boy. Rafe's dead. We got half the loot. Go back for the other half and you won't never get the chance to spend it.' Cropper John lifted the second sack. Not a full haul, perhaps, but it was enough to keep them in hooch for some time.

The young tearaway was boxed in, unable to move. He thrashed some but it was no use. They had him penned in.

'Let's get outa here before them critters organize a posse,' urged Otero.

Eddie allowed himself to be hustled away, the raucous cheers from the citizens of Tularosa ringing in his ears. He cast a bleak eye back towards the scene of death.

'You scurvy dogs ain't heard the last of this.' A tight-lipped hiss escaped from the twisted mouth. 'Not by a long chalk. Nobody gets the better of a Clayburn and lives to brag about it.'

With the town marshal lying dead, no rational consideration about the formation of a posse to pursue the rest of the gang took place. The buzz of excited conversation centred on the infamous outlaw gang leader who had also been downed.

'Did you see who gunned that varmint?' queried one avid bystander.

'Didn't get a chance with all the lead flyin' around,' commented his buddy.

'It was Sol Henshaw,' observed a third onlooker. 'That sure was some piece of fancy shootin'.'

'And thirty yards for a killing shot takes a sharp-shooter of some distinction. What do you boys reckon?'

Nods of approval concurred with the rather wild assessment.

'I would have said forty yards at least,' remarked Hyram Swinburn, taking charge of the retrieved sack of money. A bloodstained necker was tied around his head. 'And it only needed the one shot too.'

Sighs of admiration for such accurate gunplay

rippled through the large throng that had now gathered.

'None of us realized that you were such a good shot, Sol,' praised the banker with a beaming smile.

The injury was forgotten. His heartfelt praise was all the warmer for the fact that most of the stolen loot had been saved. The gang had dropped the bag containing the larger denomination banknotes. All they had got were singles and fives, no more than a few hundred dollars at the most.

'There'll be a reward in it for you and Russ to share. The bank is always generous to those who help protect its interests.'

'And there's a Wanted dodger pinned up in the law office offerin' an even grand for the body of Rafe Clayburn – Dead or Alive!' asserted Josh Waggler who cleaned out the cells.

Sol shifted uncomfortably as he shrugged off the lavish compliments. 'It was a lucky shot, that's all,' he stressed, trying to dispel the myth that was rapidly building up. 'And the guy was no more than twenty yards away.'

Laughter erupted at the storeman's obvious modesty.

'And anyway,' continued Sol, hoping to pass the undesirable glory to other shoulders. 'It was Russ Bradley who brought the horse down. He's a much better shot than me.'

'Well, one thing is for sure,' declared the bank manager. 'This deserves a celebration. Everybody over to the Pink Lady for a drink. And you two gunfighters are the guests of honour.' Then, with a sly grin, Swinburn turned to face the assembled citizens adding: 'And the bank's paying.'

Raucous cheers erupted. Free drinks were always welcome. With that most satisfying of conclusions to this grim scenario, the whispering crowd slowly drifted away. It was left to Sol and Doc Farthing to organize the removal of Mort Allerdyce and the dead outlaw.

A single tear dribbled down the tough old medic's swarthy left cheek as he arranged for the mortician to prepare his old friend for burial. It was only later that evening that Sol was able to commiserate with his regular visitor. A stronger beverage than coffee was passed across the counter. The doctor slung it down in a single gulp.

'You going over to the saloon, Doc?' enquired a gloomy Sol Henshaw.

'This ain't no time for celebrating,' muttered the distraught medic, his watery eyes misty with suppressed grief.

'My thought entirely,' concurred Sol. 'Killing a man ain't my idea of a hootenanny neither.'

Before they had any further time to discuss the incident, the shop door burst open to admit a gangly jasper clutching a notepad. He was accompanied by an assistant toting a large unwieldy camera which he proceeded to set up inside the store.

Travis Walker was the editor of the *Tularosa Tribune*. It was little more than a weekly four-page rag. But being the only paper in Sierra County, it enjoyed a wide circulation.

'I've already written down Russ Bradley's account,' declared the newspaperman. 'Now it's your turn, Mr Henshaw. And our readers would like a picture of the man who shot and killed the infamous Rafe Clayburn.'

Sol did his best to play the events down. The last thing he wanted was to be regarded as some latterday heroic avenger. But he couldn't replay what had occurred to suit his own wishes. It had happened and folks were convinced that Soloman Henhaw was a fast-shooting gunslick. All he could do was hope that the truth of the matter would be reported rather than the fantasy. Then folks would forget the unsavoury incident and get on with their lives.

It was the following day, and the gruesome occurrence was being replayed by the younger members of the community. Billy Henshaw was surrounded by 'most every kid in town. They all wanted to be friends with the son of a renowned gunfighter.

And Billy was enjoying every second of his unexpected popularity.

'Never knew your pa was such a good shot,' spluttered one goggle-eyed kid handing over a much-prized orange.

Billy deftly sliced it in half with a knife and bit deep into the succulent fruit. Juice traced a tortuous trail down his chin. He casually accepted the compliment and gift with a nod.

'Pa don't like to brag about it,' gloated the gun

merchant's son with a casual shrug. 'He says it only makes folks swell-headed when they show off their talents.'

'I bet he ain't as fast as the Ringo Kid,' sniffed a spotty youth pushing through the group. Hands on hips, he affected a display of arrogant scorn in front of Billy. His surly tone was challenging.

Billy's response was a disdainful snort. 'He'd make that turkey look like a desert tortoise,' he huffed, drawing up his slim frame. Even so, he stood a good head shorter than the challenger.

'You're lyin'. It was a lucky shot,' accused the bully, pushing Billy hard in the chest. 'Nobody's that good. Least of all some weak-kneed shopkeeper.'

The smaller boy went down. But Billy Henshaw was no coward. That much his father had taught him, along with the finer points of self-defence that Sol Henshaw had acquired in the boxing ring. And the insult to his father made Billy see red.

Spitting out a caustic retort, the glowering boy launched himself at the strutting peacock. Head lowered, Billy slammed into the boy's midriff. The momentum found both of them rolling on the ground. Dust rose in clouds. A roar went up from the surrounding youngsters as fists flailed in wild abandon. The bully was larger, a brawny tough. But like all such types, he was a coward at heart when confronted.

Nonetheless, blood had been drawn on both sides. The burly youth was quickly getting the upper hand. Only the firm intervention of Doc Farthing prevented an escalation of the conflict and serious injury being inflicted. The medic grabbed the collars of both boys and dragged them apart.

'What in tarnation is this all about?' he snapped brusquely. 'Billy Henshaw fighting in the street? Your ma would be mighty upset to see her only son become nought but a common brawler.' Then he turned to the other boy. 'And you should know better, Jack Parsons, picking on a kid half your size.' The doctor shook them both roughly, then said, 'Now shake hands and go about your business. And let's not be having any more of this ruckus.'

The two squabblers reluctantly obeyed.

'And the rest of you clear off before I call on your parents.' A quick snap of the fingers and the street was empty. All except for the medic and young Henshaw, who was frog-marched back to the gun shop.

'Let's see what your pa has to say about this,' said the croaker sternly while at the same time stifling a grin. The boy's mortified expression indicated punishment enough. And he had only been defending the gun merchant's honour. What red-blooded son would not?

'Landsakes, Billy Henshaw,' exclaimed his startled mother on witnessing the battle-scarred youth being ushered into the shop. 'What in the Lord's name have you been doing?'

The doctor threw a surreptitious wink at his friend before answering in a suitably austere tone, 'Just defending the family name is all, Maddy.'

47

'That's as may be,' countered the woman, fixing a reproving eye on to her squirming son. 'But I'll not have any boy of mine brawling in the street. In the back, young man. You're on shop chores for a week.'

As the disconsolate youngster disappeared into the living quarters at the rear of the store, the front door opened, revealing the portly figure of the bank manager. The beaming smile had been replaced by one of puzzlement.

'Thought you fellas would have been at the celebration last night,' he said. 'Russ Bradley was there, lapping up all the attention.' He sniffed upon recalling the farmer's other proclivity. 'Not to mention the free booze.'

Furtive glances fizzed between the medic and the fantasy gunslinger.

'We didn't figure it was an appropriate event to be celebrating,' remarked Doc Farthing tersely.

The barely concealed reproof passed over Swinburn's head. 'Well, maybe you will want to attend a meeting that I'm convening on Monday in my capacity as town mayor,' he said, 'seeing as it's for the appointment of a new marshal to hunt down these bandits.'

FIVE

A FATAL CHOICE

Eddie Clayburn had been hitting the bottle like
there was no tomorrow. His mood was bleak, the
dark expression clouding his flushed contours
hinted at dire consequences should anyone bug him.
Not only had his brother been shot dead, but the
take from the robbery was far less than expected.
The bag contained no more than 300 bucks.

Chickenfeed! Not even enough for a single blow-
out in Lordsburg. He growled out another savage
imprecation. The young hardcase had assumed that
command of the gang was his by right. None of the
others had voiced any objection, primarily on
account of the kid's undeniable speed with the six-
shooter on his hip.

Cropper John might have been the most skilled
shot, but he was not about to challenge Eddie. He
was aware that the others might well have voiced

their objections in that respect, him being the new guy.

Brewer was just a gopher, and Otero had no ambitions in that direction either. So on to Eddie's young shoulders fell the responsibility of leadership. And his avowed first job was to rub out the bastard that had killed his brother. Nothing took priority over that. And the more he drank, the greater became his need for revenge.

It would have to be soon.

No matter that the others were more concerned about planning their next job. That would have to take a back seat until Eddie's fervid obsession was satisfied. Family loyalty demanded nothing less.

Slippery Dom had been gone for four hours. Eddie had dispatched him to the nearest settlement to obtain a copy of the latest edition of the *Tularosa Tribune*. He was certain that a robbery in which the local tinstar and a outlaw with a price on his head had been killed would merit a special print-off.

He was not wrong.

Brewer arrived back late afternoon. He was indeed brandishing a newspaper. Eddie grabbed it. And there on the front page was the grim headline. Etched starkly in heavy black print, it read *Notorious outlaw shot by town heroes*. Eddie grounded his teeth in fury as he read the lurid details.

Adding insult to injury, there was a dual picture of the two so-called *heroes*. He threw the paper down.

'Fix yer peepers on to them murderin' skunks, boys,' he growled. 'Because on Monday, we're gonna make that town wish it had never tangled with the Clayburn Gang.'

The new gang leader's narrowed eyes blazed with a fiery resolve. A manic grin distorted his youthful contours into an ugly warp of pure hate.

Glances of indecision shot between the gang members. Sure, Rafe Clayburn had been a solid if rather unspectacular leader. And his sudden departure was to be regretted, especially now that his headstrong younger brother had taken up the reins of command. But they were all in this game for the profit afforded by good jobs that paid well.

Going after the killers was not something they relished. Revenge was a mug's game, especially when it was somebody else's kin. The atmosphere in the cabin was anything but congenial.

Eddie immediately picked up on their reluctance.

'So are yuh with me on this?'

His tone was brusque, challenging in its torrid delivery.

Silence.

'Any man that don't back me in avenging Rafe's killin' is a yeller rat and don't have no place in this mob.' His knuckles blanched white as he gripped the pearl handle of his revolver.

Otero was the one to voice their unspoken concerns.

'Easy there, Eddie.' His tone was mollifying, a gently calming lilt. 'No reason to go off half-cocked. It ain't that we're agin yuh. But. . . .' Otero gulped. He was no fast gun. Eddie Clayburn was not in an accommodating mood.

'Yeah! Go on!' rapped Clayburn. 'You were gonna say?'

John Beswick took up the gauntlet. 'That god-damned town will be all on edge now,' he said briskly. Eddie's blotched features glowered back at him. Seeing the young gunnie's lithe frame stiffen, John moderated the objection with a muted note of servility. 'Goin' in there on a revenge mission might bring a heap of trouble down around our necks. We all liked Rafe. He was a solid guy to have at your back. . . .'

Now it was John's turn to dry up.

Eddie surveyed the shifty group. His regard was chock-full of scorn.

'So I've inherited a bunch of greenhorn snakes, is that it? Soft-boiled mealie-mouths who ain't worth a plugged nickel.' He headed for the door of the cabin. 'In that case, I'll do the job myself. And when I get back, you varmints better not be around.' The implied threat was obvious.

'Hold on there, Eddie,' Otero called after the retreating back. 'Nobody's said we won't back you up. Of course we want to see Rafe's killers pay the price. But this thing just needs some careful planning to ensure there are no mishaps this time.'

Clayburn paused. A thin smile flickered across his handsome face.

'Does that mean you're with me?'

Nods all round.

'I knew all along that you guys would play ball,' he

crowed, squaring his slim shoulders. Then, just to whet their appetites, he added: 'And once them dirty skunks have been sent packin', there's a bank in Alamagordo that's just askin' for some smart dudes like us to pay it a visit.'

Re-energized, Eddie once again headed for the door of the cabin. The others remained seated.

'On your feet, boys,' snapped the bristling young hothead. 'It's party time!'

The Pink Lady was crammed to the rafters. Almost every man in Tularosa was present, not least because of the free drinks promised by Hyram Swinburn. Clouds of cigar smoke drifted in the yellow light cast by low-slung tallow lamps hanging from the tobacco-stained ceiling. The atmosphere was light-hearted. Everybody was in jovial spirits.

The celebration was in full swing when the bank manager called everyone to order with a sharp rap of his beer mug on the bar top.

'Listen up,' he shouted above the caterwauling din. 'We have important business to conduct tonight.'

'Ain't nothin' more important than suppin' your ale, Hyram,' called back one inebriate wit from the back of the room. Jubilant peals of drunken laughter greeted this jovial comment.

Again the banker slammed his pot down. This time, the gathering simmered down to hear what he had to say.

'As you know, our well-respected town marshal was

brutally gunned down last Friday.' The saturnine statement silenced any further mutterings as the stark reminder asserted itself in all their thoughts. The banker paused to allow the dour fact to sink in among the assembled citizens. 'So that means we need to elect a new marshal. And quickly. We can't have the town unprotected and at the mercy of other outlaw gangs.'

A murmur of agreement rippled through the sobered townsfolk.

'The question is, who do we elect?' Swinburn cast a bleery peeper around the attentive faces. 'Anybody got a suggestion?'

Men looked at one another, nudging, pointing. Various suggestions led to coarse guffawing.

Swinburn's moustache twitched with irritation.

'This ain't no laughing matter,' he rasped with indignation. 'Choosing a new law officer is a serious business. So cut the blather and let's do the job properly.'

The gathering quickly quieted as a voice from the back piped up, 'How about Sol Henshaw? He's obviously the best shot in town.'

'And the job sure needs a guy who's handy with a gun,' agreed his buddy.

Nodding heads approved the proposal as all eyes focused on the reluctant hero.

'How's about it then, Sol?' urged the bank manager. 'You up for it? The job pays well and includes a percentage of all fines exacted.'

Sol was horrified. This was the last thing he

wanted. But he couldn't just reject the offer out of hand. A myriad confused thoughts rushed through his head as the gathering eagerly awaited his response. He stood up to face the ocean of staring faces.

'It sure is an honour that you fellas think me worthy of such a task,' he began, choosing his words with care. 'But the fact is that I just ain't got the time. Running the store is a full-time job. What you need is somebody who can handle the weight of responsibility with diligence and justice.' He paused to let the import of his assertion sink into the drink-addled minds. 'And the guy you need is right here.'

Puzzled expressions followed this delivery. Giving a broad smile, Sol slapped Russ Bradley on the back. 'In my view, this brave and resourceful guy has all the right credentials to make a first-rate lawman.'

Attention shifted to the stocky farmer.

Sol gave a sigh of relief.

'Well, Russ?' enquired Swinburn. 'What d'you say? Do you want the job?'

Russ was slower in his reactions than Sol, not least because he'd consumed far more liquor.

'You're a crack shot with that rifle.' The banker looked to the crowd. 'Ain't he, boys?'

Strident hollers of enthusiastic agreement followed.

'I ... well, I ... hadn't given it much thought,' stuttered the bemused dirt-spreader, his soused brain attempting to get a grip on what had been proposed. He scratched his head, eyes rolling in confusion. The job paid a sight better than dirt-farming. And it was less back-breaking. Then there was the prestige, his added standing in the community. The grim fact that he would have to go after the Clayburn Gang passed unheeded.

Cheers and the insistent appeals of the crowd pressed in on the dazed farmer. He found himself carried along on a wave of euphoric hysteria.

'Yeah, why not?' he agreed, contriving a bleary smile. 'OK, Mr Swinburn, I'm your man.'

'Well done, Russ. Or should I say . . . Marshal.' Cheers all round. 'And just to show this ain't no practical joke, here's the icing on the cake.' With that announcement the bank manager, who also happened to be town mayor, pinned the badge of office on to the new lawdog's shirt. 'We'll settle the details in the morning. And now that we've sorted out the official business, let's get back to the important stuff.' Swinburn turned back towards the bar and shouted, 'Set 'em up again, barman.'

As one, the assembled hoard surged across to crowd the long bar. Only Sol remained seated. He had no wish to celebrate what in effect had been an accident, a stroke of pure luck. Quietly, he slid towards the door of the saloon and hurried off back to his rooms above the gunshop.

Had he been a touch more observant, he would have noticed a group of riders entering the town from the east.

Eddie Clayburn was in the lead. He had no fear of

being recognized. Dark shadows of night blurred their faces which had in any case being masked during the robbery. The boisterous festivity drew them ever closer to the Pink Lady. After tethering their mounts outside the four men peered into the saloon through the front window.

At that moment a drunken reveller stumbled out, knocking into the hovering outlaws.

'Hold up there, partner,' hollered Clayburn catching the man before he fell to the ground. 'What goes on here?'

'Ain't you heard?' slurred the tottering inebriate. 'We've just appointed us a new marshal.' He slung a thumb towards the raucous gaiety within. 'Drinks are on the bank. But you'd best be quick. That old skinflint Swinburn won't be payin' up all night.'

'This lawdog got a name?' cajoled Cropper John.

'Russ Bradley,' replied the swaying man. 'He's the guy that shot down that scumbag what tried to rob the bank.'

Eddie Clayburn's eyes narrowed to red pinpricks of hate. His body tensed as the lethal gunhand searched for the ivory butt of his pistol. Otero stepped quickly forward to prevent any premature unravelling of their plans.

'Where does this jasper live?' he pressed the drunk.

'Russ has a farm six miles east of town near Mescalero,' burbled the lurching fellow.

'Much obliged, mister,' Otero replied, gently nudging the man on his way. The drunk staggered off down an alley to relieve himself.

Eddie whipped out a copy of the *Tularosa Tribune* and studied the pictures of the two men who had thwarted their recent endeavour. A thin tapering finger stabbed at the depiction of the grinning mush of Russell Bradley.

'You'll soon be smiling at the devil,' he snarled acidly.

Meanwhile Brewer had been paying close attention to the celebrations inside the Pink Lady. His keen gaze focused on the bulky form propped up against the bar, a raised glass in one hand, surrounded by the cheering throng.

'Could that be the guy?' he enquired of Clayburn.

The gang boss joined him to compare the grainy black-and-white image with reality.

'Sure as eggs is eggs,' he averred. 'And now we know where he beds down, we can wait for him to ride home. Then . . .' he paused. Slowly but with firm deliberation he drew his gun and aimed it at the swaying form inside the saloon. 'That's one murderin' toad who'll bite the dust.'

'Come on, boys.' Eddie stepped down into the street. 'We got us an ambush to set.'

SIX

ONE DOWN. . . .

It was another hour before the steady drumming of hoofs assailed the ears of the waiting bushwhackers. Lack of any cover had forced the gang to arrange their surprise reception committee closer to the town limits than they would have liked. Silvery light spilling from a brazen half-moon hadn't helped matters either.

The very last building on the eastern edge of Tularosa was an abandoned cow byre. It was smelly and full of dung, but would have to suffice.

The hazy form of a single horseman hove into view. He was swaying ungainly in the saddle. Humming a tuneless ditty, the guy was totally unaware of the imminent danger into which he was riding. Luckily for the bushwhackers, he was alone. Eddie's brutish face split into a mirthless smile. This was going to be more simple than he had reckoned.

Once the rider had passed the last building, the gang quickly emerged from cover and surrounded him.

The man's eyes rolled as he attempted to make sense of this unexpected encounter.

'Some'n you fellas want?' The slow drawl, slurred by an over-indulgence of liquor, bore no hint of alarm.

It was Eddie who replied. His own low-pitched query crackled with menace. 'Are you Russ Bradley, the new tinstar?'

'What if I am,' responded Bradley, suspicion rising in his dry throat. 'Who wants to know?'

'Only the guy whose brother you shot and killed,' hissed Clayburn, drawing his pistol. 'Now it's your turn, sucker.'

Bradley's eyes widened. His hand reached for the gun stuck in his belt. But the new marshal was no gunslinger and stood little chance against the vengeful outlaw.

Orange tongues of flame belched forth, lighting up the night sky. Bradley threw up his arms, the stocky frame tumbled over the back of his mount. Eddie Clayburn continued to fill the punctured torso with hot lead. A ugly grin of macabre pleasure accompanied the lethal injection. Only the click of the hammer on to an empty chamber stayed the angry fusillade.

Snatching the newspaper from inside his jacket, Eddie scrawled a black cross over the face of Russ Bradley and threw it down on to the corpse.

'One down, one to go!' he growled, dragging his horse away from the cold-blooded carnage he had so recently perpetrated.

It was now time to hit the trail. And Lady Luck was on their side.

At that precise moment the taunting face of the gleaming moon was obscured by a bank of cloud. Darkness, black and concealing, enveloped the macabre scene. Pounding hoofs burned dust as the Clayburn Gang disappeared into the night.

Back in the Pink Lady, the festivities were still in full swing. Yet even the jovial clamour could not muffle the sharp reports of gunfire from outside. Bleary eyes turned towards the muted sound that echoed around the room. Puzzled frowns creased numerous foreheads as soused brains tried to make sense of this capricious interruption to their celebrations.

'Who's firin' a darned pistol at this time of night?' enquired one disturbed voice.

'Could be some jasper pottin' at the moon,' suggested another drinker, trying to make light of the menacing volley. Restrained laughter followed the attempted witticism. But it lacked any jollity.

'Maybe we oughta investigate,' proposed the bartender, looking round for support.

'Ain't that the job of the marshal?' came the instant reply.

'But he ain't here.'

'And he only left a short while ago.'

Slowly, the significance of these two recent events

began to impinge on the rapidly sobering throng. Was there a connection? Surely not.

The door of the saloon crashed open. A red-faced man stood there; his heavy breathing indicated that he had been running. He pointed up the street in the direction in which Russ Bradley had so recently departed.

'It's the marshal!' he exclaimed sucking in huge lungfuls of air. 'He's been shot.'

Gasps all round. Boots shuffled uncomfortably on the wooden floor as men looked askance at one another. All thoughts of the free drinks standing on the bar top were forgotten. This was serious. Russ Bradley had only been marshal of Tularosa for less than an hour, and already he had been gunned down, likely shot dead. What was happening?

It was left to Hyram Swinburn to take charge.

'Somebody go fetch Doc Farthing,' he shouted, pushing his way through the heaving mass of bodies. Reaching the door, he addressed the sweating messenger. 'You best show us where this vile deed took place.'

With less than eager anticipation, the reticent crowd made its faltering way up the street.

'What's all the fuss?'

Sol Henshaw had been unable to sleep.

An ominous sense of guilt clutched at his stomach. To avoid awakening his slumbering wife Sol had repaired to the small kitchen at the rear of the second-storey apartment to brew a fresh pot of coffee. The fact that Russ Bradley had no experience of the dangerous situation into which he had been thrust weighed heavily on the storekeeper's mind.

Maybe he should have agreed to take the job. Although he couldn't deny that a man whose sole knowledge of firearms was in their marketing stood little chance of being a successful law officer.

This blend of conflicting emotions tumbling around inside his head was rudely interrupted by the flurry of gunfire from outside. It had come from the far end of the main street. As with the gathering in the saloon, he was puzzled as to its source at that time of night.

'That's just what we're hoping to find out,' replied Swinburn without slowing his measured pace.

Sol joined the banker. The ominous trembling in his muscles told him that bad news was in the offing.

The muttering from the crowd stilled as it neared the edge of town. Their steady advance wavered. Then they saw it: a huddled lump in the middle of the trail, giving the appearance of a discarded bundle of clothes. But this was no mislaid laundry bag.

'It's the marshal all right!' announced the banker, his voice tight with suppressed anguish. A distinct gasp rose from those following.

'Is he dead?' came the hushed enquiry from one of the crowd.

Doc Farthing pushed through the tightly packed throng and bent down to examine the still form. The moon suddenly appeared, bathing the grisly scene in a pale wash of ghostly light. A large patch of congealed blood surrounding the body drew another tight gasp from the crowd.

Slowly the medic stood up. In a voice, cold and leaden, he declared, 'Some of you guys carry him down to the undertaker's. There ain't nothing I can do for him now.'

'Look at this,' said the bartender of the Pink Lady holding up a copy of the *Tularosa Tribune*. He pointed to the depiction of the two men. That of Russ Bradley had been crossed out.

It took a couple of minutes for the full significance of the defacement to register. Then slowly, as one, all eyes shifted to the man whose features remained unsullied. Sol Henshaw's feet shuffled uncomfortably.

Doc Farthing quickly noted the fear sweeping through the gathered citizens of Tularosa. One down, one to go. And maybe more before the gang were satisfied that their thirst for vengeance had been assuaged. Such emotive feelings needed countering rapidly to prevent panic taking over the town.

'There's nothing any of us can do tonight,' he shouted above the rising tide of anxious grumbling. 'Go back to your homes. I suggest that the town council summon a meeting in the morning to discuss the matter. Then it can be decided what's to be done to hunt down the perpetrators of this odious crime.'

Nobody moved. Shock had set in.

'You heard what Doctor Farthing said,' snapped Hyram Swinburn, clapping his hands for attention.

'This is no time for arguing the score. As mayor of Tularosa, I agree with his view on the matter. We can't do anything now. Pass it round that all town officials should gather in the council rooms above the bank at ten o'clock sharp in the morning.'

Harsh claps of thunder rolled across the bleak wilderness of the Malpais as the new day dawned, an ominous sign that Tularosa was in for a period of uncertainty. The steady beat of rain pummelled the shingle roof of the two-storey bank. Any discourse within the council chamber had to be raised in volume for all to hear what was on offer to allay their fears.

Following an hour of sharp-tongued dialogue, little of any weight had been achieved.

The brutal slaying of Russ Bradley, barely more than an hour into his tenure of office, had unsettled everybody. And as a consequence, nobody was willing to take the job on. The council meeting had been full of hot air, and little else.

By the end of the meeting the job still remained vacant. All that had been suggested was that an emissary be dispatched to the nearest major town, Socorro, in order to seek out a suitable alternative.

Skip Logan, who ran the livery stable, was adjudged to be the best rider in town. After being summoned by a messenger, the guy was given his instructions.

'You can offer up to double the usual payment,' stated the mayor, while casting a regal eye over the

65

gathering. Nobody challenged the decision. Higher taxes were a small price to pay for peace of mind. 'But it has to be somebody who can handle a gun and isn't afraid to use it.'

'We don't want no mean-eyed gunslinger pinning on a badge,' appended the undertaker, Jed Rankin. 'The town has to have a proper lawman.'

'Good lawmen are hard to find,' answered the young liveryman lighting up a quirly as he walked over to the door. 'I can only see what's available and make my own judgement.'

'Ride like the wind, Skip,' urged Swinburn. A sense of panic caused his voice to crackle nervously. 'The town's counting on you. We don't want to be left unprotected longer than is absolutely necessary.'

'All being well, I should be back in a week,' Logan stressed.

'Hopefully with a suitable candidate in tow,' stressed the undertaker. A murmur of subdued agreement followed the young horseman as he left the meeting.

'Good luck to you, Skip,' encouraged the doctor as the door closed. 'You're going to need it.'

Six days had passed since the ostler departed for Socorro.

The sun, which had shone brightly from a cloudless sky, was fading towards the sculpted skyline of the San Andreas Mountains. The storm had passed, and with it the sense of fear of retaliation from the Clayburn Gang.

Skip Logan was due back on the morrow. He would, everyone hoped, be accompanied by a new man to administer justice. And then the killers of poor Russ Bradley could be hunted down and accorded the full rigour of the law.

Nothing untoward had occurred in the meantime to suggest that Tularosa was anything other than a somnolent range town. Slowly, life was getting back to normal. As with all similar situations, the passing of time tends to favour a return of confidence.

But all was not as it seemed.

Maddy Henshaw, for one, was more than a little worried. The defacing of the picture of Bradley gave an unspoken message that could not be ignored. Her husband tried to make light of the incident, assuring his wife that a new lawman who was experienced in these matters would soon catch the culprits.

But Maddy was not convinced.

'That paper was deliberately left to tell us those killers will be back to complete the job.' Her voice was thick with emotion. As she wrung her hands a worried frown furrowed her brow. She tried to keep busy, aimlessly moving stock around the shelves in the store. 'What we gonna do about it, Sol?'

The pleading tone in her voice tugged at her husband's heartstrings. He knew the way his wife's mind was working. But Sol Henshaw was a stubborn man. There was no way that a bunch of outlaws was going to drive him out of his home. He had made a good life for himself and his family in Tularosa. And he would fight tooth and nail to retain it.

'Skip will be back tomorrow,' he breezed, infusing a heavy dose of optimism into the declaration. 'Then we can rest easy knowing that a proper lawman will be inaugurated to protect us.'

'Sol's right, Maddy,' concurred Doc Farthing, who had been playing patience alone in the corner now that his old buddy had so abruptly shed this mortal coil. 'And I'll make darned sure that he hires a couple of deputies to strengthen his hand.'

'There you are.' Sol forced a smile. 'Everything's going to be fine. You'll see.'

With both men bombarding her with fervent reassurances, the dark cloud hanging over Maddy Henshaw's beatific countenance slowly began to lift.

'If you say so,' she murmured somewhat diffidently.

'We surely do.'

This emphatic response was uttered in unison. Both men laughed. Maddy joined in although not fully convinced that once again the future was looking rosy. She lit one of the oil lamps. The warm glow helped to soften the tense contours of her face.

'I'll go fix supper,' she said, smoothing down her apron. She headed for the stairs at the rear of the store.

The medic continued with his game of patience.

SEVEN

IRON MIKE STEEL

Neither Sol nor the medic knew that Skip Logan had already returned from his trip to Socorro. He was accompanied by a hard-bitten jasper who went by the name of Iron Mike Steel. The ostler headed directly for the bank, eager to inform the mayor that his trip had been a success.

Skip had been in Socorro for three days before happening upon Mike Steel. He had been all set to abandon his quest having drawn a blank with regard to the hiring of a suitable candidate to sport the marshal's badge.

The sheriff had been of no help, claiming to be short-handed as it was. No way would he permit the newcomer to make an offer to one of his deputies. Skip was left in no doubt what would happen should he go against the lawman's ruling.

'So what do you suggest I do, Sheriff?' he

lamented. 'Tularosa needs a town marshal.'

'There's plenty of guys down at the Gaslight who would jump at the chance with what your council is prepared to pay.' Clem Ganley jabbed a finger at the young ostler, fixing him with a beady eye. 'But I'll warn you again. Approach any of my boys and I'll stick you in the hoosegow and throw away the key. Got my drift, fella?'

'Loud and clear, Sheriff.' Skip sighed and made for the door. 'Where can I find this Gaslight dive?'

'Down the street aways, you can't miss it,' Ganley said without looking up from the Wanted dodgers he was sorting.

Treating the uncooperative lawdog to a venomous scowl, Skip slammed out and paced up the noisy street. At least the sheriff had been right. You sure couldn't miss the Gaslight saloon. Unlike many such establishments, it was illuminated more brighly than a Thanksgiving Day firework display.

As he pushed through the door, his ears were assailed by a raucous din. Everybody seemed to be shouting above the noisy rendition being pumped out by the house band at the far end of the narrow room. Hunched over a beer at one end of the long bar in the Gaslight, Skip began surveying the dense throng of patrons for a likely person to approach with his offer.

By his third night at the Gaslight all offers had been turned down. Either the jaspers he approached were soon judged by him to be two-bit gunslicks, or they were otherwise engaged. If he failed tonight then he would have seriously to consider heading east to Fort Stanton. But that would mean having to cross the dreaded white sand desert of the Malpais.

Skip had only been in the saloon for a half-hour on his third night, and was on his second beer when he noticed a cluster of onlookers watching a high-stakes game of poker. Of the four players, two had dropped out leaving the house dealer and a tough-looking though well-dressed jasper, sporting a thick black moustache. More distinctive, however, was the flashy red silk vest.

In the middle of the green baize table sat a large pile of bank notes. The dealer was smirking as he waited for black 'tache to make his play.

A few gentle enquiries revealed that the dude was called Iron Mike Steel, a visiting gambler who was losing heavily. Steel was down to his emergency poke. This hand was his final chance to turn the tables and get his money back. For five minutes the gambler had been studying his cards.

The general hubbub in the saloon had simmered down to a low rumble as more and more punters surrounded the table. There must have been a cool grand in the pot. Thin tendrils of smoke writhed in the hot atmosphere, like a phantom nest of hungry rattlers.

The Mexican house-dealer was becoming impatient.

'You gonna play or fold, mister?' he snarled, bearing a set of yellowed teeth.

Iron Mike's response was a tight smile. He turned

to address the watching patrons.

'Who'll give me odds on this greaser' – he paused, allowing the insult to sink in before pointing a casual thumb towards the hovering gambler – 'having a pair of threes up his sleeve.'

Puzzled frowns greeted the offer. So Mike enlightened the onlookers.

'He swapped them for a pair of aces that had somehow jumped out of the pack and into his hand during one of those special deals. It took me a while to figure it out.' Mike leaned forward. 'Am I right, four-flusher?' He uttered the challenge with a menacing hiss.

The gambler snarled. Jose Carrera had been playing the scam all week since getting the job of resident cardmaster. Now he'd been rumbled. And there was no escaping the threatening growls from irate bystanders who had already been fleeced. There was only one way out of this situation.

Kicking over the table, the house-dealer lunged backwards, grabbing for the small Colt Lightning tucked away inside his jacket.

Coloured gambling chips and greenbacks flew about in wild abandon. The crowd of angry punters shrank away, eager to view but not be a part of the violent confrontation.

Iron Mike was ready. He had been expecting such a move.

His right hand reached behind his neck and grasped the bone handle of a Bowie knife tucked away out of sight. In a single fluid motion, he launched the deadly blade just as the pistol was emerging from the gambler's jacket.

Such was the force and speed of Iron Mike's manoeuvre that the gambler found himself being punched backward, his body skewered to the wall. There he hung, blood draining from the fatal injury. Jose Carrera would not be cheating any more unfortunate customers.

Mike scooped up the wad of notes off the floor.

'Sorry about that, folks,' he declared cheerily as if the deadly incident was nothing more than a minor irritation.

Setting his hat straight, the natty gambler smoothed down his vest and brushed a fleck of dust from the black suit before sauntering across to the pinioned corpse. Offering it a look of contemptuous disdain, he then casually levered the blade from the wooden slat. The dead body slid down the wall, leaving a red smear in its wake. Bending down, he wiped the knife clean before slipping it back into its sheath.

'OK folks, the show's over,' the gambler hollered above the burbling commotion that the sudden and violent incident had engendered. 'Everyone over to the bar. The drinks are on me.'

A loud cheer greeted this welcome announcement. The cheating house-dealer was forgotten in the stampede.

Skip eventually managed to corral the popular cardmaster, edging him over to a vacant booth. After sticking a fresh drink in Steel's hand, the young ostler then proceeded to deliver his job proposal. Great emphasis was placed on the enhanced payment that the position promised.

No mention, however, was made of the true reason as to why the vacancy had arisen. Skip claimed ignorance on that issue, explaining that he was merely the messenger delegated by the town council. All would be revealed once they reached Tularosa.

Iron Mike received the offer with nonchalant ease.

'Well, it so happens, Mr Logan,' he stated casually, 'that I am indeed between employment at the present time. So your proposition will suit my current circumstances admirably.'

'I take it you are as handy with a revolver as you are with that pig-sticker hanging down your back.' Skip's searching eyes flicked towards the bone handle jutting out of its custom-made holder. It was a statement rather than a question, Skip naturally assuming that the gambler was proficient in all areas of personal protection.

'Indeed I am,' Steel answered, somewhat aggrieved at the implication of any doubt. 'This little beauty has done me proud on numerous occasions in the past.' A twin-barrelled Deringer pistol appeared in his hand, as if from nowhere.

Skip's florid visage creased in hesitancy.

'I was talking about a six-shooter and rifle. A marshal has to be able to uphold the law and be able to—'

'I know what it means, fella,' interrupted the gambler acidly, his face registering indignant scorn at the insinuation. 'How'd you figure I got nick-named Iron Mike? Jim Bowie sitting on my back, and this little guy, are merely there to give me the edge. If your town council can supply me with Sam Colt's latest arsenal, then I'll make use of 'em. Savvy?'

'S-sure thing, Mr Steel,' stammered the contrite ostler, 'No offence was intended, I can assure you.'

Steel's response was a curt nod. 'Then you got yourself a deal,' he replied thrusting out his hand.

Skip Logan accepted not quite knowing whether he had done the right thing.

After introducing Iron Mike Steel to the town council, Logan made a swift exit. The mayor was rather less than impressed with the potential badge-toter. But the gambler was all they had. Nobody else had come forward willing to take on the infamous Clayburn Gang. And once he had been informed that this was to be his prime task, Iron Mike had demanded that his already substantial fee be doubled.

Argument and remonstrations raged back and forth as Hyram Swinburn attempted to threaten, wheedle and coax the gambler into withdrawing his objectionable demand.

Mike just sat there, smoking a large Havana cigar and picking his nails with the large knife. A thin smirk lifted the corners of his mouth as the war of words continued.

Then he stood up.

'Suit yourselves, gentlemen,' he breezed, heading

for the door. 'I could probably make just as much operatin' the tables in the Pink Lady over the street. That place looks like it could use a hot dealer to liven things up around here.'

The announcement effectively quieted the blustering dignitaries.

'No need to be hasty, Mr Steel,' exclaimed the mayor, throwing anxious glances at his fellow councillors. 'I am sure we can accommodate your request providing, of course, that you will guarantee to rid us of this vengeful gang of brigands.'

'Ain't nobody can make that sort of pledge, Mayor,' Steel replied. 'But I'll do my best. So what's it to be?'

Nobody spoke.

'Well, I'll be in my room over at the hotel when you decide.' With a flourish he swung on his heel and was gone.

Darkness shrouded Tularosa's main street.

The front of Henshaw's gun store lay in deep shadow. The only source of light was the small lamp at the rear, where Doc Farthing was ensconced. Maddy headed for the stairs leading to their private quarters to prepare the evening meal. Her husband lingered, not wanting to leave the old-timer who still visited the store regularly. He really missed his deceased buddy.

'Fancy another coffee, Doc?' Maddy called over her shoulder.

'I'll get us a couple of Havana cigars,' added Sol

following close on his wife's heels.

'Won't say no to a slice of that apple pie as well, if'n you've a mind,' came the pleading voice from over in the shadows. Man and wife grinned at one another.

Doc Farthing was nothing if direct. His request elicted another wry smile from the woman's radiant face.

'Maybe you'd like to stay for supper as well?'

'Wouldn't say no,' came back the gruff though appreciative response.

'Figured that might be the case,' answered Maddy Henshaw, chuckling. 'Lucky I put on some extra vittles.'

The ageing medic then resumed his game. A muted sigh escaped from between pursed lips as his watery gaze drifted towards the now unused chessboard.

The dim light cast by the lamp only just reached to the table where he sat. His hand leaned over to adjust the wick of the lamp.

But he never got the chance to effect the change.

EIGHT

. . . . AND ONE TO GO

Outside, silvery rays from a spectral moon filtered through the patchwork of cumulus cloud creating a shadowy world of flickering images. The shifting shadows that flitted about the town harboured their own menacing agenda. Two shapes emerged from the gloom and paused at the north end of the main street.

Eddie Clayburn had opted for the gunhand, Beswick, to accompany him on his mission of revenge. The others had been left to kick their heels at the cabin.

The gang leader's eyes fastened upon the gun store. The newspaper article had been more than generous in describing where the other 'hero' of the foiled Tularosa bank robbery carried on his business.

Extra caution had to be observed. Henshaw being a gun merchant, Eddie automatically assumed that this critter would be no tenderfoot in the shooting department.

Keeping to the shadows, he waited until the street was empty before nudging his mount forward. Beswick followed ten yards behind, gun in hand. This was Eddie's play. He was there merely as back-up, just in case.

Eddie reined in to halt a block down from his objective. A light burned in the store window. Careful not be seen, he dismounted and gingerly stepped up on to the boardwalk. After a brief look around he sidled along the edge of the shop fronts.

Arriving at the gun shop, he paused to draw breath and still his pounding heart. Tight-lipped, nerves taut as banjo strings, he slowly hauled out his revolver and cocked the hammer. The sharp double click sounded like the ripple of castanets in the still night air.

He peered round the edge of the window frame into the shop's interior.

A quick scan revealed that nobody was tending the counter on the left side above which the oil lamp hung. No problem. He rapped on the door with the ivory butt of his gun.

A muffled voice inside called out, 'I'll get it.'

The scraping of a chair was followed by a blurred shadow approaching the door from the right side of the store. All the man outside could see was the vague outline of a dark silhouette.

Eddie tensed, the knuckle of his trigger finger white. Judging the man to be about to open the door he fired. Four shots shattered the silence. A brilliant plume of fiery orange belched forth. Glass flew inwards as the bullets found their mark. The dull image staggered and cried out.

The killer's mouth split in a taut smile. Not waiting to verify the accuracy of his shots, Eddie scuttled back to his horse, which Beswick was holding in readiness for a fast getaway. He knew instinctively that the target of his gunplay would not be getting up. He leapt into the saddle and vigorously lashed the animal into a frenzied gallop back down the still empty street.

The two gunmen were quickly swallowed up by the Stygian gloom and were well beyond the town limits before anyone realized what had occurred.

The direful sounds had brought Sol Henshaw hurrying downstairs from the upstairs living quarters. The two cigars in his left hand split apart under the pressure of a clenched fist. Halfway down the steep flight of steps he drew to a sudden halt. At the bottom, her dress stained a bright red, lay Maddy Henshaw.

Sol gulped. Eyes bulging wide as dinner plates, his mouth flapped open in horror. For what seemed an hour, in fact no more than five seconds, he stood there, rooted to the spot, transfixed by the appalling vision.

A groan from the splayed out form brought him back to the gruesome reality of the situation.

'Thanks be praised!' he cried, realizing that his wife was not dead after all. He leapt down the steps to cradle her in his arms, gently brushing the tangled locks of auburn hair off her ashen face. The woman's eyes slowly flickered open.

'W-what happened?' she murmured, her voice weak and faint. 'My . . . arm feels like . . . it's . . . on fire.' The halting delivery brought a cruel twist of agony to the smooth complexion.

Sol ignored the question. He knew what had happened. The nocturnal visions of hell that had invaded his dreams since the shooting of Russ Bradley had now become an even more dreadful reality than he could ever have imagined.

Could things get any worse?

And where was Doc Farthing?

'Hey, Doc!' he hollered, his vocal chords rasping with anxiety. 'What's keeping you? Maddy's bleeding bad over here.' He waited impatiently. But there was no reply.

Then young Billy hurried in to the store from the street. He had been staying with a friend and heard the gunfire. Before the boy could ask what had happened, he tripped over something blocking the doorway. He cried out.

'Is that you, Billy?' shouted Sol. Without waiting for an answer, he rapped out, 'Go find Doc Farthing. The old buzzard must have gone for a leak out back. And be quick about it. Your ma's been shot.'

A tortured wail of terror burst from the boy's lips as he realized that it was the old medic's body that

81

he had tumbled over.

'He-he ain't out back, Pa!' Further words stuck in Billy's dry throat.

'What you burbling about, boy?' snapped his distraught father. 'Your ma needs medical attention quickly.'

Billy gulped hard as he stumbled away from the frightful corpse.

'He's been shot, Pa. And I think he's dead.'

A choked gurgle issued from between clenched teeth as Sol took in the awful reality of what had occurred. The emotional pain hurt far more than a punch in the guts. Those bullets had been meant for him. And, to make matters worse, his wife had taken a stray.

Suddenly the dire situation into which he had so unwittingly been pitched had become a whole lot worse.

The staccato rattle of firearms had set off the local dogs. Strident yapping rent the air, accentuating the sombre mood of fear in the dim interior of the gun store. Other citzens now shouldered their way into the premises.

They were led by the bank manager.

Someone turned up the lamp to reveal the grisly extent of the attack. A hoarse whoosh from a dozen intakes of breath immediately followed. Slivers of broken glass mingled with the spreading pool of blood oozing from the doctor's fatal chest wounds.

The apprehensive group shuffled their feet uncomfortably.

Hyram Swinburn quickly shrugged free of the frozen immobility that had seized him as he took in the scene and its implications, especially for himself.

His rotund features hardened, beady eyes narrowed to thin slits. He shook his head. This menace couldn't be allowed to continue. It boded ill for the town. These bandits were hell-bent on revenge at any cost. They had turned the quiet enclave of Tularosa into a battleground.

But, most important, folks would take their business elsewhere unless something drastic was done. He was not by any means convinced that Iron Mike Steel would live up to his tough nickname. The guy was a gambler by profession, not a lawman.

The banker's steely gaze fastened on to the sorry form of the storekeeper who was gently rocking to and fro, clutching the blooded body of his injured wife.

Swinburn didn't try to conceal the anger that twisted his rotund features into a scowl. This was all Henshaw's fault.

It was he whom the gang wanted, yet others had become the victims. First Russ Bradley, and now Doc Farthing. Even Maddy Henshaw had been caught in crossfire. Who would be next? For as sure as night follows day, it was clear that the Clayburn Gang would be back once they learned of yet another mistaken killing.

And they would be madder than a wounded grizzly.

Something had to be done.

Swinburn squared his shoulders. An icy mask replaced the paralysed lineaments of shock. He had made a decision. And he was certain that the town council would back him to the hilt.

He threw the bulky envelope clutched in his right hand on to the counter. He had been carrying it over from the bank when the sudden outburst of gunfire had driven him back into the relative safety of a nearby alleyway. Only when he was certain that any threat of further gunplay had receded did he emerge tentatively from cover.

Drawing himself up to his full, if rather diminutive height, the banker coughed before speaking.

There was no hint of sympathy evident in the terse delivery that followed. 'This here envelope contains the reward due to you for the killing of Rafe Clayburn. It amounts to fifteen hundred dollars.'

Swinburn's delivery was flat and darkly ominous. Raised eyebrows and muttered comments accompanied the surprise announcement. He paused for effect before continuing.

'Since Russ met his end, the whole caboodle comes to you.' He paused to draw breath and gird himself for the final declaration. 'I know it ain't your fault, Sol,' Swinburn's voice faltered now that he was about to deliver the uneasy proposition, 'but as mayor of Tularosa I have to think of the bigger picture, the greater good. You understand, don't you?'

It was a wheedling plea that received no recognition in the gun merchant's bleak regard. Sol's face assumed its own hard lines. He knew exactly what was coming here, but had no intention of making it easy for the odious critter.

'What is it you have to say, fella?' he rasped.

The banker hesitated. Then fear of what he perceived would be the likely consequences should he back down now took control. He coughed nervously before continuing in more composed tones.

'The town council feels that this money is enough for you and your family to start up elsewhere. I personally will ensure that you receive full compensation for this business and will furnish a letter of introduction that will enable you to get help from financial institutions wherever you decide to settle down.' He waited for the import of his generous offer to sink in.

Others around him nodded in agreement.

'Sounds fair to me,' averred one bystander. Others concurred with barely vocalized mutterings.

Outside, an owl hooted imbuing the dismal proceedings with its mournful tone.

Sol remained tight-lipped.

Purposefully, his frosty gaze panned the room. A barely audible hiss of derision issued from his lips. Then, without uttering a word, he stood up and turned his back on the gathering. Embellishing the act with a suitable flourish of contempt, Sol carried his wife upstairs. Halfway up, he paused, swung round and addressed the gaping horde in a nonchalant tone of voice.

'I'd be obliged if one of you gentlemen would arrange for the doc's body to be carried over to the undertaker's.'

Then he was gone, followed by a thoroughly chastened young Billy Henshaw.

The mayor also made a hasty exit. His destination was the hotel. He now realized that the council had little choice but to accept Iron Mike Steel's terms of employment.

NINE

THE LEOPARD CHANGES HIS SPOTS

Carefully laying Maddy on the bed, Sol examined the wound. He was relieved to note that it was only a minor gash. The bullet had dug a shallow groove in her upper arm. But it could easily have been much more serious. That was the reason why he had arrived at the regretful decision that his wife and son must be sent back to live with his father-in-law in Nebraska. At least until this business had been sorted out.

'You go put some water on to heat up,' Sol called to his son. 'We're gonna have to do our own doctoring for a spell.'

After Billy had left, Maddy took hold of her husband's arm. There was a surprising degree of strength in her grip. Fixing a poignant eye on to the

87

scarred features that loomed before her, Maddy posed the question that had been bothering her.

'Are you going to take up Hyram's offer?' she asked. A pleading urgency was reflected in the limpid pools peering up at her husband. 'For us all to leave here and start afresh someplace else.'

'Part of it,' was the hesitant reply, the gun merchant feeling unable to meet her worried gaze.

Maddy frowned. 'And what's that supposed to mean?'

'It means that you and Billy are leaving. You can stay with your pa in Broken Bow until—'

'And what about you?' Maddy interposed anxiously.

'I'm staying to see this thing through.'

Maddy raised herself up on to one elbow. Shock was etched on her pallid face.

'You are no gunfighter, Sol Henshaw,' she said shaking his arm with a surprising vigour. 'These men will be back once they learn that another mistake has been made. And figuring to face down hardened outlaws with your fists is no answer. They'll be mad as hell and like as not shoot up the town. Others could be killed. That's why Hyram Swinburn is so worried. And that's why we all have to leave while we still can.'

'All that weasel is concerned about is his own hide,' grumbled Sol.

'But what he said makes sense,' countered his wife.

Sol had no reply to such forceful logic.

Though outwardly he displayed a stoical calm, Sol's mind was in turmoil. He stood up and walked over to the far side of the room where he stared hard at the mirror's uncompromising reflection.

The hollow-cheeked outline that peered back was drawn and tired, moulded by the results of innumerable past conflicts in the boxing ring. It was not a pretty face. For some minutes he just stared, fighting an inner battle with his demons.

Ought he to leave now, run away?

There could be no denying that he was a novice where gunplay was concerned. But he could learn. Run now and he would always be looking over his shoulder. Eyeballing every roughneck who scowled at the world, he would be forever quaking in fear as to whether this was the guy who would finally ventilate his craven hide.

That was no way to live.

A man should be able to defend his family with honour so that they were proud of him. Not ashamed. And that's what Billy would feel if'n his pa fled the battlefield. Nought but a yellow coward.

So his mind was made up. A new firmness settled about the taut jawline. A firmness that spoke of a solid resolution not be thwarted from its purpose.

He reached in to the drawer below the accusing mirror and removed a tooled leather shellbelt, complete with holster in which rested a pearl-handled Colt Frontier revolver. It was the latest model from the revered gunmaker's factory in St Louis.

Sol's thoughts drifted back to his meeting with the colonel's son at a convention he had attended earlier in the year. The founder of the company had died in

1862 but the reputation of his wares had been enough to ensure its future success as the most renowned gun manufacturer in the country, if not the world.

Not all of those present at the gathering were supporters of the right to bear arms. There was a vociferous delegation of women representing the anti-gun lobby. When challenged, Colt junior had poured scorn on their claims by asserting that his guns were *Peacemakers*, expressly designed to preserve life by helping to resolve disputes as quickly as possible.

A further contention: that if every man had a revolver on his belt nobody would dare draw first, was delivered somewhat tongue-in-cheek. The Western frontier was full of stories recounting gun duels that had ended in death. Nevertheless, Sol had been impressed enough with Colt's reasoning to keep one of the free samples which had been locked away in his private drawer – unseen and untouched.

Until now.

He had been intending to put it on dislay in the shop window. For some unaccountable reason he had delayed.

A faltering hand caressed the leather and the smooth blue of the steel barrel. Maybe his mind had already been made up following that first killing of the marshal. Perhaps the brutal realities of life in a wild and untamed land had forced him to bury his moralistic objections and face the truth.

Slowly and with deliberation he fastened the

deadly firearm around his waist and tied down the retaining strap.

Maddy's eyes widened in horror. A shaking hand covered her gaping mouth.

'You can't,' she cried struggling to rise. 'They'll gun you down in cold blood.'

But there was no strength in her limbs. She turned away when he tried to kiss her, tears in her eyes. No words were spoken as the wound was cleaned and dressed. Billy didn't cotton to the sudden chilly atmosphere that had invaded the room. His own thoughts were subdued, blunted following the recent spate of violence.

Next morning, over breakfast, the atmosphere in the cramped upstairs apartment had thawed. The undying love that both Sol and Maddy felt for each other overcame any discord. During the uncomfortable night, each had made the decision to accede to the other's wishes.

It was Sol who broke the ice.

'I've been thinking,' he began tentatively. 'You're right. I cannot hope to compete with a gang of hard-boiled gunmen. We'll accept Hyram's offer and go back to Nebraska. Maybe your pa will take me on again.'

Maddy smiled. Her hand reached out across the table and grasped that of her husband. Their eyes met.

Then she slowly shook her head.

'No Sol,' she whispered. 'It's you who's right. I was being selfish and thoughtless. We have to meet this threat together. This is our home and nobody is going to force us out. Neither skulking outlaws, nor our self-serving neighbours.' Maddy squeezed the heavily calloused hand. 'And I'll be proud to stand at your side.' She paused, a lump blocking her throat, 'Whatever the outcome.'

'I don't want you getting in the firing line, gal,' Sol emphasized, 'but if you're sure this is what you want. . . .'

'That's my decision and I'm sticking by it.' Maddy's resolute assertion was clearly defined in the stubborn set of her flushed cheeks. Sol knew not to dissuade his wife once her mind was made up.

'I'm also here to support you, Pa,' cried young Billy laying a protective arm around his father's trembling shoulders. 'The Henshaws against the world.'

A tear formed in the corner of Sol's right eye. He quickly brushed it away. This was not the time for displays of emotion. His head drooped. Then he shook off the fleeting moment of weakness. His son wanted – needed – a resolute and determined father now more than ever.

Sol repeated his son's contention with a measured degree of firm deliberation. 'The Henshaws against the world.'

He clapped the boy on the back. Then, with more sanguinity than he had felt of late, he threw him a broad smile.

Billy responded gingerly. 'Does than mean you'll teach me how to fire a gun, Pa?'

The query, which Sol ought to have anticipated,

effectively terminated the brief period of accord. As a greenhorn in the gunfighting stakes himself, Sol was in no position to provide the required tuition even if he had chosen to do so.

In this both parents were united.

'Me strapping on this rig don't alter anything, son,' he told Billy, glancing towards his wife for her support.

Maddy took the hint.

'Your father is right, Billy,' she agreed, holding the boy by the shoulders and fixing him with a determined look that brooked no rebuttal. 'It don't change the fact that you are still too young for such things. And in any case, I need you here to help me run the store.'

The boy's face fell. But he accepted the decision with tight-lipped stoicism.

'Now go on out and play afore I have you mucking out the stable.' A wide smile illuminated the crestfallen boy's face. The threat was sufficient to launch the boy towards the door. 'And mind you don't get into any more fights!' Maddy's final light-hearted admonishment was lost as the door slammed shut.

A bleak cast settled over Sol's careworn features as he picked up the Colt revolver manual and leafed through its pages. This was something that had been forced on to him.

And so, displaying a measure of melancholic reluctance, he kissed his wife *adios*. 'I'd best head over to Caballo Canyon and learn how to operate this durned thing,' he sighed. 'Nobody goes there and it's hemmed in enough to dull the sound of gunfire.'

Then he headed for the door leading down to the back lot. He did not want anybody seeing him depart and wondering. Prying eyes would lead to questions he had no desire to answer.

TEN

UNEXPECTED HELP

Four days passed, with Sol leaving each morning as dawn was breaking to avoid being spotted and possibly followed. His return at noon was easier to explain away. The problem was that he was no marksman, Even following the gun owner's manual to the letter, he was still only hitting one out of every six tin cans set up as targets.

His draw was slow and clumsy. If only these critters didn't carry guns, he could easily have handled them. But there was no point wishing and hoping for something that would never happen. Sol's shoulders slumped in dejection as another chamber-load of bullets kicked up dust but nothing else.

He sat down on a rock, the empty pistol forgotten as he contemplated a bleak future.

How could he defend himself against hardened gunmen whose sole aim was to put him in boot hill?

Maybe he ought to surrender to the inevitable and leave Tularosa. But slinking away, tail between his legs like a beaten cur, went against everything to which Sol Henshaw had ever aspired.

Even during a title fight against Mad Dog McGurkin, when Sol had been floored three times in one round, he had never given up. The bookmakers figured they had made a killing as all bets for a win had been laid on Battling Solomon King. Peering through swollen eyes at the leering brute, Sol had come out for the final round and pummelled the critter into the canvas.

The silverware and winner's rosette now rested on the dresser in the apartment above the store. They were his proudest possessions. There had to be a way to beat these skunks.

A rattle of shod hoofs on stone broke into his downcast reverie.

His first thought was that someone had stumbled upon his secret, or maybe followed him. The rider trotting down the narrow canyon was easily recognizable as the dandy new marshal. Sol had met him the day following the murder of Doc Farthing. It was obvious that the guy was a gambler and was merely filling in time as a lawman until a better opportunity arose.

Still, at least he must be able to use a gun. Unlike some.

'So this is where you come to try out the new delivery, Mr Henshaw.' The wry smirk creasing the lawman's face said everything about what he thought of the gun merchant's prowess with his wares. 'It appears as though you are a better salesman than a shootist.'

Sol shrugged. 'I wasn't aiming to hit anything,' he reciprocated while reloading the Colt Frontier from a box of cartridges. 'Just checking they all work properly, is all.'

Iron Mike was not fooled.

He had been apprised of the dire circumstances that gripped Tularosa and, in particular, one of its leading citizens. He handed the latest copy of the *Tularosa Tribune* across to the 'gun tester'. It was hot off the press that morning. And there on the front page were the lurid headlines in stark black and white, together with adjacent pictures of both the deceased and the intended victim.

Even with no solid proof, the report took the view that it was a case of mistaken identity. Sol Henshaw had to be the one whom the killer was really after. It was his store that had been shot up, and he was the one who had shot and killed Rafe Clayburn. Revenge is a potent motivator.

The damning report laid emphasis on the gun merchant being a perilous magnet that would bring the robbers back until such time as their bloodthirsty lust for retribution was sated. And by stubbornly refusing to leave Tularosa, he was, in effect, holding the town to ransom.

So there it was. Out in the open. He had become a pariah, a wretched outcast through no fault of his own. Now he knew why people had begun to avoid him and had stopped coming into the store.

His teeth ground in frustration. Maybe he should leave, after all. Was it fair to put the rest of the town in jeopardy on account of his male pride? Iron Mike appeared to read his thoughts.

'Don't go and let that dumb piece of horseshit scare you,' he said gruffly, nodding at the article. 'A man has to stand up for what he believes is right. And one of these beauties will give you an edge.'

He removed a Loomis shotgun from the specially made scabbard fixed to his mount's saddle. The barrel had been cut back to no more than eighteen inches. He handed it to Sol.

The gun merchant had numerous long-barrelled versions on display in the store. But he had never come across one like this. He looked blankly at the marshal.

Steel walked across to the untidy heap of tin cans and built them up into the shape of a pyramid on top of a boulder.

Making sure he was well beyond the line of fire, he then ordered Sol to pull back the twin hammers and point the double-barrelled shotgun in the general direction of the new target.

'In your own time, mister,' said the lawman, smiling, 'but keep a firm grip on the stock. These guys kick like a mule.'

Sol arced the short barrel towards the target, held his breath, then pulled the trigger. The gun roared. Smoke poured from the twin exits. When it had dispersed, there was no sign of the target. It had been completely demolished. Shattered tin cans lay strewn about the sandy bed of the narrow canyon, bent and pitted by the lethal discharge.

The marshal couldn't restrain a raucous chuckle of delight.

'Heehaw!' he sang out. A broad grin split the creased visage. 'So what d'yuh think of that then?'

Sol was speechless. His head nodded in amazement.

'Yeah,' was all he could manage.

'Now ain't that the answer to your problem?'

Again Sol nodded. 'I guess so,' came the surprised rather mesmerized response. 'I never figured these type of guns could be so . . . destructive.'

The marshal went on to explain the principle.

'Shortening the barrel allows the shot to spread over a wider area. But you do sacrifice distance which means you have to be closer to the target. All the same, it makes the ideal weapon for a guy that . . . well . . . ain't too hot on accuracy. Just point the critter and fire. It'll remove anything in the way. Permanently.'

At last Sol found his voice.

'I sure am glad you happened to mosey on by, Marshal,' he said gratefully. 'I was figuring to up sticks and disappear after my dismal efforts to become a gunslinger.' He paused momentarily scratching his head, his face assuming a pinkish hue of chagrin. 'Fact is, I ain't never fired a gun before that day the bank was robbed. Everybody reckons that being a gun merchant, I must be a marksman.

That's why I came out here in secret.' He threw the lawman an anxious glance. 'You ain't gonna split on me, are yuh?'

Marshal Steel gave the nervous query a perfunctory guffaw.

'Don't you fret none, fella,' he said with solid assurance. 'Your subterfuge is safe with me.' The tin star hooked his thumbs in the dandy red vest, his face affecting a thoughtful expression. 'Old Iron Mike has a few dodges of his own that are best kept from public view.' He threw his companion a wink, tapping his nose artfully. 'If'n you get my drift?'

The problem for Sol was that such modified arms like Steel's Loomis were not advertised for sale in any reputable firearms catalogue. Not illegal as such, they had to be custom altered by an expert metalsmith.

Steel noted the pensive frown as Sol handed back the deadly gun. He could see the dilemma facing the gun merchant.

'Tell you what I'll do,' he said, offering the gun back to Sol. 'You keep this here cut-down in exchange for a brand-new one from your shop. That way I can get it altered by the blacksmith without any suspicion being aroused.' Steel held out a gloved hand. 'Do we have a deal?'

'Why not,' replied Sol. 'This dude can by my equalizer.'

'And rest assured that I'm in the process of hunting down those murdering critters. That's how I came upon you out here in the wilds. So I'd best be off doing my job. *Adios*, Mr Henshaw. And make sure to keep a tight hold of that cannon. As you've just discovered, it packs a mean punch.'

Sol's reaction was a sardonic smile.

'I know all about them, Marshal,' he muttered slamming a bunched fist into the palm of his left hand.

The lawman answered the comment with a wry twist of the lip but didn't pursue it. Then he mounted his cayuse and swung round to depart. 'While Iron Mike Steel is toting the lawman's badge, the citizens of Tularosa can rest easy. I'll make sure they know it.'

Soon the lawman had disappeared from view to continue his quest.

Sol's unexpected meeting with the new lawman had raised his spirits. For the first time since this unsavoury business had been unwillingly thrust upon him, he experienced a new confidence surging through his veins. The feeling was good.

But Iron Mike Steel was not all he appeared.

A gambler at heart, he was no tracker and knew that he stood little chance of hunting down a gang of desperate robbers. Nor had he any intention of so doing. The new marshal had a healthy respect for maintaining his own skin intact.

The fulfilment of his legal obligations necessitated an outward display of bravado that he was well adept at carrying off. Performing the mundane tasks of a small-town badge-toter posed little difficulty for such a wily and devious character.

Only when the gang made their move would he need to reassess the situation. A louring grimace cast a shadow across the profile of the gambler's grizzled face as he cynically eyed the newspaper report. This might well be the push that would tip the Clayburn Gang over the edge. Discovering they had killed the wrong man was not likely to leave them in the best of moods.

A ripple of trepidation filtered through the new lawman's normally resolute frame. Iron Mike Steel felt his hardened muscles turning to jelly. He could always just leave the territory, disappear. Then the thought of all that easy dough drifted across his blurred vision. And he had not yet been paid.

He shrugged off the brief period of uncertainty.

ELEVEN

BAITING THE TRAP

Slippery Dom Brewer was adjusting the leathers on his saddle when the pounding of hoofs drew his attention. Beswick had gone to the Orogrande Trading Post for a copy of the latest edition of the *Tularosa Tribune*. Eddie was especially eager to read up on the events surrounding their most recent foray into the town.

Brewer frowned. Judging by the dust he was kicking up, Cropper John looked like he had a burr up his ass. The rider skidded to a grinding halt in front of the secluded cabin and leapt from the saddle.

'Why yuh in such an all-fired hurry?' questioned Brewer.

Beswick ignored him, hustling straight into the cabin, a copy of the news sheet clutched in his hand. He threw it on to the rough plank table in front of Eddie Clayburn jabbing a finger at the all-important column and upsetting a mug of coffee in the process.

'Read that!'

Eddie glared at the gunman whose ragged appendage had assumed a darker hue.

'Read it!' the hardcase repeated grabbing hold of a nearby whiskey bottle and tipping a liberal slug down his throat.

The other members of the gang quickly gathered round, drawn by the harsh intonation of Beswick's outcry. All eyes dropped to the lines of print. As he read, Eddie's eyes widened and his lower jaw fell open as he took in the awful truth.

Then he exploded out of his seat. The whiskey bottle was flung against the fireplace, smashing into a myriad slivers and staining the grey stone a dirty brown. Stalking round the small room, Eddie stamped his boots on the news sheet that now lay on the earthen floor of the cabin.

'That damn blasted turkey has more lives than a cat,' he railed. 'I'll get even with that no-good varmint, if'n it's the last thing I do.' Eddie's staring eyes burned with a manic ferocity.

Still not satisfied, he then drew his pistol and vented his anger even further against the offending item, only ceasing when the hammer clicked on to an empty chamber. The clamorous din stung their ears making the silence that followed almost palpable.

But it did serve to calm the irate gunman to a degree where his associates could make a tentative attempt at communication.

As usual it was Otero who pointed out the hazards of a hells-a-poppin' frontal assault on the town.

'They have a new lawman installed,' he voiced cautiously. 'And the town's gonna be on edge and likely to haul off at any strangers that show more than a passing interest in their luckiest citizen.'

Eddie scowled. 'So what we gonna do?'

Cropper John provided the solution.

'We need to get this new tinstar and a posse out of town.'

'And how do we manage that?' snorted their peevishly impatient leader. 'Invite them all out on a Sunday picnic?'

Beswick managed to keep a cool head with difficulty. His leaden gaze fastened on to the snarling young gunnie.

With slow deliberation, he plucked a black cheroot from his vest pocket, scratched a vesta on the scarred table and lit up. Blue smoke curled and twisted into a perfect line of rings, one following after the other like a herd of sheep. All the while, an unblinking stare held the bristling young gunman.

Only then did Cropper John deign to outline his plan.

'We lure them out by robbing the Artesia stage when it passes through the Sacramento Mountains. The monthly payroll for the Penasco mine is due to pass through Capitan Pass in two days. That's no

more than a half-day's ride from Tularosa. It sets off
from the mine's head office in Alamagordo at six in
the morning. If we reach the pass by noon, that will
give us an hour to set things up.'

Otero greeted the suggestion with a sceptical
glower.

'How come you know so much about payroll ship-
ments?' he demanded.

'I was workin' out the details when me and Rafe
met up. That was gonna be the gang's next job. One
man couldn't handle it alone, which is why I agreed
to join up. But then the poor guy got himself shot.'

A sombre melancholy settled over the group.

Then Eddie's face lit up. 'Well, this job will be ded-
icated to his memory. Rafe would have liked that.
And I like it too.'

Beswick's face cracked in a lurid smile as he continued outlining the rest of the strategy.

'Once the guards have handed over the strongbox, we let slip who we are and that we're headed for
the Mexican border. The wagon is certain of return-
ing to Tularosa because that's where the nearest law
is to be found. Ain't no doubt that the marshal will
want to investigate the scene of the crime. And while
he and his danged fool posse are chasin' all over the
country, we'll sneak back into town and do the business with Rafe's killer.'

Beswick leaned back, a superior look challenging
the others to throw out any objections to the venture.

Nobody spoke for a while as they each considered
the merits or otherwise of the proposal.

All eyes swivelled towards Eddie. As leader it was his prerogative to voice the first of any comments.

The young gunman chortled at the notion. 'That gullible badge-toter will be leaving Tularosa wide open, makin' sure that we won't have any trouble. My brother, God rest his soul.' Automatically the fiery young tough crossed himself before continuing. 'He sure knew what he was a-doin' of when he met up with you, John.'

Eddie reached over for a fresh bottle of hooch and cracked it open, passing the hard liquor to Beswick. 'And this time we'll make darned sure of finishin' the job.'

Once again it was Otero who posed a question that seemed to have been omitted from Beswick's detailed explantion.

'A hefty payroll is gonna be well guarded. You thought of that, Cropper?' The chunky stalwart leaned across, his stubbly chin jutting forward.

Beswick merely shrugged.

'We'll make certain to be holdin' the high ground and have the element of surprise on our side.' He smirked and pumped out another cloud of smoke. 'That suit you?'

'It sure suits me,' replied Clayburn. 'And some'n else.'

Suddenly Eddie's stubbly features crinkled in delight. His back stiffened. He'd had an unexpected brainwave.

'What if we do the double?'

The others waited. Otero sighed, barely able to

conceal his exasperation. What was the vengeance-crazed jasper about to propose now? Eddie didn't heed the warning glare. His whole being was focused on the unparalleled scheme he had just cooked up.

To rob the Artesia stage, then hot-foot it back to Tularosa and empty the bank.

Faster than a roadrunner, words clipped with passion and racing ahead of his tongue, Eddie blurted out his plan. To his knowledge nothing like that had ever been done before. Eventually he paused to take a breather, assisted by another gulp of hooch.

'Pull this off, you guys,' he whooped with vigour, jabbing a grubby finger at the open-mouthed bunch, 'and the Clayburn Gang will become famous throughout the territory and beyond.'

The gang leader's glassy eyes assumed a remote cast as his thoughts described the prestige that such an accomplishment would bestow upon him. Eddie glowed with satisfaction at the notion. His brother would be jealous as hell sitting up there now. For what seemed an eternity nobody spoke.

Then Otero voiced another objection. 'What's to say this Henshaw dude won't join the posse?'

Beswick provided the answer. 'Most lawdogs only sign up men with no commitments. Why should this dude be any different?' He smiled. 'That satisfy you?'

Otero shrugged.

A brief spell of thoughtful musing followed as the plan was considered. Then the normally slow-witted Dom Brewer voiced his opinion.

'That sure is a good plan, boss,' he concurred. 'And there'll be nobody left in town to cause any trouble.'

'You got it in one, Slip,' chuckled a thoroughly animated Eddie Clayburn basking in the kudos even though it was Beswick who had actually thought up the original plan. 'And don't forget there'll be twice the take. We can retire after this caper, boys. Just think of it. No more jobs payin' chickenfeed.'

He held out his hands, urging their approval of the twofold plan. 'So what d'yuh say?'

The others peered at one another, each seeking the agreement of his confederates. There were no wavering glowers of indecision. Cropper John sunk another hefty slug of whiskey, once again struggling to contain his frustration with this big-mouthed jughead. Swallowing his anger, the burly gunman made the conscious decision to quit this tinpot outfit once *his* job had been pulled.

But for now he was prepared to toe the line and give Eddie all the credit. After due consideration of all the angles he was, indeed, forced to admit that there did not appear to be any drawbacks.

Outside, a bullfrog croaked as if exhorting them to a positive judgement.

Even Otero was impressed. For once, it appeared, his wayward master had come up with a premier scheme that would keep them all rolling in clover for a considerable time to come.

As one, the gang nodded their head in agreement. Eddie Clayburn rubbed his hands. At last he was going to see an end to this dark period of his life, emerging victorious and with money to burn.

Otero shielded his gaze from the glaring orb of the sun as he hooked out the solid gold hunter pocket watch. It read a half-hour before noon.

They had made good time from the hideout in Coyote Canyon. Puffballs of white cumulus drifted by overhead. For once the blazing globe of orange was being held in check.

Capitan Pass was a narrow gorge with plenty of cover afforded by an array of tumbled boulders on either side of the trail.

From the west a series of hairpin bends forced any wagons down to the pace of a desert tortoise. This was the direction from which the payroll shipment would be approaching. At the opposite end, a gently shelving downgrade took a direct line east to cross the desolate salt and sagebrush plain of the Hondo Sink.

It offered the perfect spot for an ambush.

'OK, boys,' breezed an upbeat Eddie Clayburn, dismounting behind a large flake of red sandstone, 'One last smoke, then we get into position.'

The others followed suit, ground-hitching their mounts.

Before lighting up, they assiduously checked that their revolvers and rifles were fully loaded. It was an essential practice that had become instinctive. Each man's life depended on his own weapons functioning effectively.

With a half-hour left to go before the wagon was due, Eddie called across to Otero.

'You and Cropper take the far side. I'll set the ball rolling from here with Dom. We don't give them any chance to surrender.'

His piercing regard held each man in turn.

'And remember what I said,' he continued sternly. 'Only the driver will be left untouched. He's the one who can thank his lucky stars for being spared to raise the alarm. Drill down all the rest. None of them must leave here alive. This job will stir the blood, make the critters so mad that the law will easily recruit a large posse to follow us down to Mexico.'

A round of brittle laughter followed this comment.

'The poor saps will be so durned eager to catch us, they'll forget their damn blasted town has been left wide open.'

'And that's where we step in, eh boss?' added the beaming Slippery Dom.

'You can bet your bottom dollar we do.' Eddie smirked. 'OK, boys, this is it. And make every shot count.'

With that final piece of stimulation, the gang dispersed.

Fifteen minutes later the sharp crack of a whip announced the arrival of the wagon. It was an open flatbed with raised sides. The all-important strongbox was secured by chains in the middle. There were four guards in the back with another sitting up front beside the driver.

Eddie allowed a thin smile to cross his face when he observed that the guards were somewhat less than alert. Indeed, they were smoking in a relaxed manner, without a care in the world. Their guns were stashed out of sight on the floor of the wagon.

A macabre leer, warped with expectation, wrinkled the outlaw leader's face. This was gonna be like takin' candy off of a baby.

He threw a glance towards the far side of the pass. Cropper and Otero were well hidden. As the wagon drew closer, Eddie took a bead on the guard sitting up front. He was the only one who appeared to be doing his job. His finger tightened on the trigger of the Winchester.

The first shot ripped the silence apart, the stentorian crack echoing off the opposite wall of the pass.

It took the guard in the chest, punching him clear off the wagon. That was the signal for all hell to break loose. A continuous volley of shots poured into the occupants of the wagon. They didn't stand a chance. Not one of them even managed to raise his gun and return the withering rain of fire that had so conclusively assailed them.

The brutal attack was over in seconds.

Only the driver remained unscathed. As soon as the ear-shattering blast faded away, his hands reached skywards.

'Don't shoot!' he yelled. 'I ain't gonna give you guys any trouble.'

Eddie was the first to emerge. His Winchester pointing unerringly at the driver's chest, he approached the

112

wagon followed immediately by the others.

'Don't make a move if'n you wanna remain in one piece,' rasped the gang leader, jabbing the rifle with menacing intent.

'S-sure, mister,' stuttered the terrified man. 'Anything you say.' Big Bill Carver had no intention of jeopardizing his health. His wife had just given birth to their first child. He had only accepted this job because the regular driver was sick.

'Get the box down.' Eddie threw the order to Slippery Dom, who scrambled up on to the wagon.

A look of rank distaste twisted the outlaw's blanched features as he took in the gruesome picture of carnage. Drawing his pistol, Brewer blasted off the securing chains and heaved the blood-spattered box on to the ground.

It was now Eddie's turn to use his revolver. Stepping up to the squat, iron-strapped box, he pumped two shells into the lock, which instantly burst asunder. He toed open the lid and surveyed the contents. Staring eyes twinkled with greedy relish. Packs of banknotes were stacked side by side.

'Must be all of five grand in here,' he announced barely above a whisper as the others joined him.

'Yee-haar!' cheered Brewer, tossing his hat in the air.

Even Otero was transfixed by the sight of all that dough. It was the largest heist the gang had ever pulled. Only Beswick remained aloof from the celebrations. His steady gaze never left the nervous driver.

'This handsome poke will give us a high old time

in Casa Grande,' said Eddie, deliberately raising his voice for the driver to hear.

'Can't wait to get stuck into all them purty *señoritas*,' concurred Brewer catching his leader's sly wink. 'How far d'yuh reckon the Mex border is, boss?' he added playing along.

'Can't be more'n seven days ride from here. What d'you say, Otero?'

'I woulda said more like five if'n we head due south through Texas.'

'Then we ain't got time to hang around here,' the gang leader pointed out, stuffing the banknotes into his saddle-bags. Turning his attention back to the trembling driver he stated airily, 'It's lucky for you that Eddie Clayburn is in a good mood today, fella. Else you'd have ended up like your buddies.' The gun jabbed at the quaking driver, delivering a final warning. 'But don't you be tempted to make a move to leave here for the next half-hour, get my meaning?'

The quaking guy merely nodded his compliance.

'Let's ride, boys,' hollered Eddie. 'The Clayburn Gang has got some serious spendin' to do.'

With a rowdy chorus of halloos ringing in his ears, the wagon driver was left to cool his heels.

The gang spurred off down the grade, swinging south off the main trail in the general direction of Texas. But once out of sight, Eddie led them back up through a twisting clutter of rocks, on to the mesa above Capitan Pass. Each man dismounted, crept to the edge and peered over.

As expected, once the gang had disappeared, Carver swung the wagon around and headed back west down the hairpins. The gang watched nervously from their lofty perch. The crucial moment would come when the wagon reached the fork in the trail at the bottom.

Left for Alamagordo and the Penasco mine head office, right for Tularosa and the nearest law office.

As the wagon neared the all-important fork, their nerves twanged, breath was held in tightly. The wagon drew to a halt at the signboard. The guy was undecided which trail to take. For a long minute he waited, the gang willing him to slant right.

In the distance a muted whipcrack cut through the tense atmosphere.

Left or right?

The driver chose to head for . . . Tularosa.

An audible sigh of relief escaped from four throats.

Settling down in the shade of a rocky overhang, they now had a substantial wait until the pursuing posse arrived.

Eddie posted Dom Brewer as first sentry atop the mesa.

'Any sign of dust, you let us know,' Eddie called after the gunman's retreating back. 'Cropper will relieve you in an hour.'

Brewer nodded as he made a slithery ascent of the steep gully.

To pass the time, Eddie arranged for the exact amount of the haul to be counted. It took them a half-hour, the total eliciting a round of goggle-eyed smiling faces.

'More'n we figured, boys,' Eddie murmured with a whistle of approval.

'A cool six grand ain't bad for a few minutes' work,' agreed Beswick, lying back and thinking about the spread he was planning to set up back in his home state of Texas.

TWELVE

POSSE

Sol Henshaw was sweeping the veranda outside his store. These last few days there had seemed little else to occupy his time. Business had fallen off since delivering his rejection of the town council's offer. News had got round fast. And it seemed that folk were prepared to take on a two day round trip to the Orogrande Trading Post for their supplies rather than visit his establishment.

'Morning Mrs Baines.' He smiled gingerly at the woman bustling down the boardwalk towards him.

Her head was bent in thought. Sol's cheery greeting brought her up short. Muttering under her breath, the woman quickly crossed the street deliberately avoiding him.

So that was how it was?

He had also noticed that Chuck Bradley and the other kids didn't come round any more to call on

117

Billy. The Henshaws had been ostracized. Sol gritted his teeth. At least the new marshal was on his side. And if the Clayburns paid him another visit, he would be ready and waiting with the sawn-off shotgun.

Then maybe he would leave this town, but with his head held high.

A dog butted in on his dour reflections. Its excited yapping announced the arrival of a wagon, which was being driven at a frenetic pace. Clouds of ochre dust were being churned up in its wake. And was that streaks of dried blood that he could discern splashed across the sides of the wagon?

Sol frowned. This looked mighty serious. His previous thoughts were forgotten.

Along with numerous others who had witnessed the startling arrival, he hurried across to the marshal's office outside which the wagon had rumbled to a juddering halt. The team of four were all lathered up, steam rising in a blurred fog off their quivering flanks. They had clearly been driven hard.

But why?

'What's the hurry, mister?' call one curious bystander.

'And where's all that blood come from?' urged another.

They hadn't noticed the dead bodies in the back which they had been covered with a tarpaulin.

The driver ignored the shouted queries as he stamped up on to the boardwalk and went straight into the office without knocking.

Mike Steel was trimming the edge of a large Havana cigar. Seated at his desk, he had been studying the account of rentals collected from town stores on behalf of the council. One of the perks of the job was keeping ten per cent of all money collected.

This job was proving to be far more lucrative than he had imagined.

He greeted the sudden interruption to his deliberations with a bleak glare of rebuke. 'Ain't you got no manners?' he snarled acidly. 'Busting in here like a loco mule. I don't like it.'

Then the lawman noticed that this guy was plumb tuckered out, sweating and trembling like he'd just shaken hands with the Devil. His shoulders were hunched as he desperately sucked air into tortured lungs. Following the hell-for-leather ride back to Tularosa, Bill Carver was all in.

Steel didn't need to be a sawbones to recognize that this dude was on the verge of collapsing. He sprang out of his seat and grabbed a hold of the driver before he fell.

'Take a chair, fella,' he soothed, reaching for the blackened coffee pot that was bubbling away merrily on the stove. A strong mug of finest Arbuckles would cure anything. He handed the stained receptacle to his visitor. 'Just take your time, then tell me what in thunder has happened.'

It was five minutes before some semblance of colour returned to Carver's cheeks. He pushed a hand through his greasy mop of black hair.

'Gee, thanks a bunch, Marshal,' he gasped. 'I sure

needed that. You ain't got a tot of the hard stuff to liven it up, I suppose?'

Iron Mike responded to the request with a leery smile, then dug out a bottle from the bottom drawer in his desk.

Carver's eyes glittered with approval. He took a sip.

'Aaaaaa! Even better!' came back the rapturous reaction.

'So what you so all-fired on edge over?' said Steel.

In a series of staccato responses, interspersed by periods of hauntingly brutal recall, the payroll driver outlined the horrendous events of the robbery. But it was his final assertion that really caught the marshal's attention and found him lurching back on to his feet.

'You certain it was the Clayburn Gang who are responsible for the robbery and murder of your five buddies?' the lawman pressed firmly.

Carver was emphatic. 'They were braggin' about it. And they also let slip about headin' for Mexico.'

'Then we ain't got a minute to lose.' Steel grabbed his hat and selected a Winchester carbine from the gun rack. He buckled on the brand-new tooled leather twin-rigged gunbelt for which he'd swapped the Loomis with Sol Henshaw. He still retained the Deringer but left the Bowie and sheath in his desk. He wouldn't be needing that on a cross-country pursuit.

'Hey Josh!' he hollered loudly. 'Come in here now!'

The shambling form of the jailhouse swamper appeared in the doorway of the cell block. 'What's with the barkin', Marshal?' he grunted. 'I still got the cells to wash out after those pukin' Bar X cowpokes departed this mornin'.'

'Forget that,' rapped Iron Mike impatiently. 'There's five corpses outside that need coffins. And Bill Carver here needs a bed for the night. He can sleep upstairs in my room. You look after him. The poor guy's been through the mill.'

With that, he slammed the high-crowned Stetson on to his head and hurried out of the door. A bunch of cowboys were tying up across the street.

'Anybody who wants to sign up for a posse to hunt down the Clayburn Gang, meet me in the Pink Lady in fifteen minutes,' the marshal called across to them. 'Pass it round that I need ten fully armed men.'

Not waiting for a response, Steel hurried down the main street to the livery barn, where his own mount was stabled. Although it was late in the day there was still a couple of hours' daylight before they would be forced to make camp for the night.

Sol's jaw dropped when he heard that the perpetrators of this heinous crime were none other than his arch enemies, the Clayburns. This was his chance to end their reign of terror. He would join the posse, being firmly convinced that Steel would voice no objections in view of the circumstances.

Eddie was dozing. His hat was pulled over his eyes to shield out the early-morning sun. There ought to be time enough for one of Brewer's bacon and bean breakfasts before the posse arrived – that was, if

everything went according to plan. And why should-
n't it? He had left enough clues for a blind man to
follow.

After he had eaten, Eddie struggled to his feet and
began pacing up and down beneath the huge overhang of rock, a mug of coffee in his hand.

Time passed slowly. Too slowly for the young tearaway who was chafing at the bit.

'Take it easy,' muttered Beswick. 'They'll be here
soon enough. You can count on it.'

Eddie was about to answer the remark with a
caustic retort when Otero slithered down the loose
scree of the gully.

'They're climbin' the hairpins,' he panted. 'I
counted ten in the posse.'

'Right, boys,' prompted their leader, emitting a
coarse guffaw. 'This is where we watch a bunch of
chuckleheads chase after their tails.'

He threw the empty mug away and mounted up,
leading the others along a meandering deer trail that
wound up to the mesa overlooking Capitan Pass.

Ten minutes later the posse hove into view. They
were riding in single file. In the lead was Marshal
Mike Steel. Somewhere in the middle Sol Henshaw
peered around uncertainly from beneath a flat grey
plainsman. Louring cliffs of red sandstone rose up
sheer on either side of the pass.

The perfect spot for an ambush.

As the posse drew nearer to the waiting outlaws,
Beswick pushed his head forward. Eyes screwed up to
thin slits, he stared hard at the leading rider. Slowly,

in disbelief, his gaze opened wide. Surely it couldn't be? Cropper John shook his head, clamping his peepers shut before refocusing.

There was no mistake. There was the gaudy red vest, the high-crowned Stetson with its telltale beaded Commanche hatband.

Iron Mike Steel!

Beswick's left hand strayed to the throbbing rag of his mutilated ear. His face became suffused to a violent shade of purple, his lips twisted into an ugly snarl of defiance. After five years he'd finally met up with the bastard. Well, he wasn't about let this turkey just ride out of his life now.

But what to do? The plan was let the posse ride off in the direction of the Texas border, and then continue onward to Mexico.

Now that he'd got Steel in his sights, there was no way that Cropper John Beswick was about to let him escape the retribution he deserved.

The posse had stopped just below where the gang were secreted. The marshal stepped down and examined the empty strongbox. He nodded to the others, confirming that this was clearly the site of the robbery. Teeth clenched tight shut, fists bunched into warped lumps of bony tissue, Beswick watched his hated enemy point out the direction in which the posse would head next.

All the outlaw could think of was getting his revenge. Everything else paled into insignificance. The robbery, the bank at Tularosa and Clayburn's own manic desire for retribution were nothing compared to this. Cropper John's whole being was focused on the destruction of his enemy.

Once the posse had departed, Eddie indicated that it was time for them to move off in the opposite direction.

Beswick deliberately hung back. He wanted to be the back marker. A plan had quickly formed in his devious brain. After five minutes, he called out for the gang to stop.

Dismounting, Beswick said, 'This darned nag seems to be limping.' He made to check the back hoof, then nodded sagely. 'It's as I figured, boys. The critter's picked up a stone. I'll need to dig it out.'

Eddie grunted his irritation at the delay. 'We ain't got time for no hangin' around.'

That was what Beswick wanted to hear.

'You fellas carry on without me,' he asserted, injecting an apologetic tone into his suggestion. 'I'll catch up soon as I've sorted it out. Shouldn't take long.'

Eddie nodded his agreement. Without any further discussion on the matter, he spurred off down the trail, followed by the rest of the gang. Nobody looked back. Just to be on the safe side, however, Beswick waited until they were out of sight before mounting and retracing his route over to the far side of Capitan Pass.

He surmised that Steel would figure that the gang had at least a four-hour start. So he would not expect to run them to earth until the following day, riding at a steady canter. Beswick's spurs dug deep into the flanks of his cayuse to gain maximum speed in order to reach a suitable place for the ambush he planned. Taking out that bastard Mike Steel was all he cared about.

If he could find a place of concealment overlooking the trail where the cliffs were sheer, it would allow him to escape from the scene of conflict safe from any chance of pursuit. Removing any of the other posse members would be a bonus.

The opportunity he was seeking soon presented itself.

An extended wall of rock, unbroken as far as the eye could see and a hundred feet above the trail, offered the perfect spot to pick off his quarry. He lay down on the flat slab and peeped over the rim. And he was only just in time. The line of riders had rounded the end of the butte and were heading south between stunted clumps of cholla cactus and catclaw.

Beswick's face creased in a grin lacking any semblance of humour. The bright-red vest offered a target that was impossible to miss. He thumbed back the hammer of the Winchester and jammed it into his right shoulder.

'After five long years, it's payback time at last,' he growled. 'Nobody gets the better of John Beswick and dies in their bed. It's boot hill for you, sucker.' He drew in a large breath and held it. His trigger finger tightened. Then. '*Adios* . . . Marshal!'

The rifle bucked, a hunk of lead streaking towards its goal. Two more followed in rapid succession. All three hit their mark, ripping Iron Mike's chest apart and blasting him out of his saddle.

Beswick rubbed his torn ear. It felt better already. The constant dull ache had departed. Vengeance had been meted out. A huge weight had been lifted from the gunman's shoulders. And it felt good.

Taken completely by surprise, the posse milled about in a confused mayhem. With their leader removed from the scene, they were like headless chickens. Two more posse members bit the dust before Sol Henshaw seized control.

'Take cover in those rocks.' The gruff command emerged as a strident bark as he leapt from the saddle, lunging towards the untidy cluster of boulders opposite the rock wall. 'And don't forget your rifles.'

Grateful for some kind of authority figure to take command, the other survivors quickly followed suit. They dived head first behind the rocky shelter as more bullets pinged and ricocheted all around.

'Who in tarnation is tryin' to kill us?' shouted the panic-stricken voice of Jed Rankin, the undertaker.

'Don't matter none,' Sol rapped out. 'Just get them guns operating. Aim for the smoke of his rifle.'

The masterful presence of Sol Henshaw had saved lives. It also helped focus the attention of the posse on challenging their assailant's advantage of surprise and height. Soon a blaze of gunfire was peppering the top of the mesa where Beswick was concealed. The withering broadside forced the outlaw to duck low.

Having accomplished his self-appointed designation as the avenging angel of death, the bushwhacker returned to earth with a bump. His whole being had been focused on wreaking the ultimate reprisal for his damaged ear. For a brief period, it had left him with a dizzy feeling of euphoria. It was the culmination of years in pursuit of a demon that had poisoned his soul.

Now he began to absorb the consequences of his deranged obsession. Tackling a full posse single-handed had been the act of an unhinged mind. Sure, he had taken out his hated enemy and two others. But seven still remained, and they had quickly reformed.

Their co-ordinated retaliation following the ambush had taken Beswick by surprise. The outlaw had expected the posse to degenerate into a disorganized rabble once their leader had been removed: a mindless pack of donkeys he could pick off at will.

But these guys were like a swarm of maddened hornets. Some dude had clearly grabbed the reins.

Beswick hugged the ground as the ferocious assault on his position continued at an unrelenting pace. He was grateful for having secured the advantage of being in a position where they could not get at him. And he had the satisfaction of having achieved his purpose. Nevertheless, he knew that it was time to leave. Only a single lucky ricochet was required to put him out of action.

Keeping close to the rough ground, the outlaw slithered down the back slope to where his horse was tethered. Jagged stones tore at his jeans, drawing streaks of blood. But the outlaw didn't notice, so intent was he on distancing himself from the scene of combat.

THIRTEEN

NO LUCK FOR CROPPER

Fifteen minutes passed without any further gunfire erupting from the lip of the mesa.

'Hey, Duke!' Sol called out to a guy known for his oversized headgear. 'Raise that ten-gallon on the end your rifle and see if'n it draws any fire.'

The man called Duke Montana nodded. Slowly the large hat rose. He moved it from side to side. But there was no response, except for a cactus wren perched on a yucca and contemplating this strange new creature. Jed Rankin then did the same thing. Still no reaction.

It appeared that the bushwhacker had carried out his odious task and sneaked away like the cowardly rat he was. Another five minutes passed before Sol tentatively emerged from cover. Clutching the rifle which he had fired for the first time, Sol took a deep breath and stepped out into the open.

Silence.

The others then followed.

Sol's narrowed gaze scanned the serrated rimrock, nervously searching for any sign of movement. Thankfully there was none. The guy had definitely cleared out. His thoughts were racing. Who in their right mind would ambush a posse of ten men? Some crazy drifter out of his head, or. . . ?'

Then a notion focused itself in his spinning brain. Could it have something to do with the payroll robbery? Why else would anybody be out in this god-forsaken wilderness, waiting on a posse to just happen by? But why hang around Capitan Pass when the gang could be well on their way to the Texas border by now? None of it made any sense.

But the more he ruminated on these questions the more he became convinced that the Clayburns were somehow involved. And if that were so there was no doubt that they were driven by their determination to get rid of Solomon Henshaw.

Then another thought struck home.

Tularosa was now virtually defenceless. The marshal was dead, together with two of the best shots in the county. Could this robbery have been a devious ploy aimed at sending the posse on a wild-goose chase?

But why not just let them head off into the wide blue yonder. It was a heap safer than mounting an ambush against ten well-armed men.

There was only one way to find out the truth of the matter.

He turned to address the others who had been securing the three dead possemen to their horses.

'I'm figuring that something ain't right here,' he posed thoughtfully. He went on to explain his cogitations, finishing with the decision he had arrived at. 'There's only one way to find out what's going on and that's to split the posse.'

Frowns of uncertainty gathered across the brooding features of the six remaining members of the posse. They were all tough frontiersmen but this ambush had rattled them all. Not least Sol Henshaw. Resolutions had to be made and they all now looked to him for guidance.

'Duke,' he said, directing his orders to the cowboy, who had now replaced his large sombrero. Montana was the ramrod for Hank Lomax's Flat Iron ranch. 'You take three men and head for the trading post at Orogrande. If these varmints are aiming to cross the Texas border they'll likely call in there to stock up on supplies. Commanche Joe's place is the last watering hole before they cross into Mexico. He will know if'n the Clayburn Gang have gone through that neck of the woods.

'The rest of us will head back for Tularosa with these poor dudes.' He slung a thumb at the bloodstained bodies tied across their saddles. 'My hunch is that the gang have backtracked and are aiming to do some serious damage to the town, which could involve robbing the bank.'

This supposition received a host of sceptical grunts.

'Two robberies in one day?' declared one doubting Thomas. 'Ain't never been done afore to my knowledge.'

'There's always a first time,' rasped Sol curtly. 'And I ain't taking no chances.'

He omitted to add that his own family would be in the firing line once the gang realized that yet again their prime quarry had eluded them.

'What if Joe ain't seen them?' quizzed the ramrod.

'That'll mean my hunch was correct and we've been hoodwinked. What I can't figure out is who that bushwhacker could be.' Sol scratched his head. 'Don't make no sense that the gang would try a stunt like that.' His brain fizzed and rumbled, desperately trying to fathom the puzzling enigma.

'So what do we do next?' pressed Montana, whose simple view of life precluded any form of logical analysis.

Sol threw the ramrod a quizzical look. A good solid cattle man, Duke was no brainstormer. The guy was a follower, content to obey orders without thinking for himself. But, like a faithful sheepdog, he was dogged and determined to succeed in the task allotted.

'If Joe ain't seen them, you take the short cut back to Tularosa through the Sacramentos and over Sunspot Plateau,' Sol said slowly to ensure that Montana got the message. 'We can only hope that my interpretation of all this turns out to be a load of eyewash. But somehow, I got me a bad feeling.'

'We better get on the trail then,' declared Duke prodding the others to mount up. He cast a seasoned eye towards the dipping sun. 'There's still a good two hours of daylight left. We should be there by noon tomorrow, all being well.'

'See you back in Tularosa,' replied Sol with a wave of his hand.

He sighed in frustation knowing that he could not make Tularosa before nightfall. Much as he would have preferred to travel under cover of dark, the risk of injury to horse and rider in the wild and rugged terrain was too great to contemplate. And that bush-whacker might still be out there, watching and waiting for another chance to complete the job he had started.

It would be a long night for the frustrated gun merchant.

Beswick spurred off, the crackle and whine of angry lead shot ringing in his ears. If he pushed the large bay mare to full gallop, he ought easily to catch the boys up in a half-hour.

Yet still he had failed to heed what common sense ought to have told him. The wind had picked up to a stiff gust having swung around to the north west. The sound of gunfire would carry a long way.

The faint crackle of firearms had cut through the hot air of late afternoon, causing Eddie Clayburn to prick up his ears. He drew to a halt. Ottero and Slippery Dom Brewer followed suit. It had come from the direction they had recently left. His immediate assumption was that it had to be connected with the posse.

And Beswick had not yet caught them up. It oughtn't to have taken this long to dig out a stone. Putting two and two together, the obvious conclusion was that the apparently separate incidents were connected.

The outlaw leader's shrewd reasoning translated this to mean that Beswick had gotten involved in a shooting match with the posse for some unaccountable purpose of his own. Maybe they'd happened upon each other by accident? Eddie scowled. He was not convinced.

'Step down and stretch your legs, boys,' he said. 'I have me a feelin' that ol' Cropper is gonna be along soon.' His voice dropped to a menacing growl. 'And he's got a heap of explainin' to do.'

'You figure that was John back down the trail aways, boss?' enquired the lean-limbed Dom Brewer. 'Why in tarnation is the knucklehead blastin' off with his hogleg?'

'Now that's one dandy question he's gonna need a gold-plated answer for,' answered Clayburn, his beady eyes fixed on their back trail.

An hour later a spume of dust caught his attention.

'OK, boys,' he said coolly. 'Spread yourselves apart, and keep me covered. No sudden moves in case he's playin' us false.'

Ten minutes later Beswick arrived in a flurry of dust.

'You been a long time, Cropper,' Clayburn remarked with casual indifference. 'Some'n hold you up?'

'Just took longer than I figured to dig that stone out.'

Clayburn nodded, apparently accepting the explanation while lulling Beswick into a false sense of security.

Beswick didn't perceive the atmosphere of menace hanging over the clearing. 'You boys didn't need to wait on me. I'd have caught you easily.'

'It was some'n else that attracted our attention,' observed Clayburn, the oily hint of a smile still pasted on to his face.

Beswick waited, oblivious to where this was heading. It was Otero who filled him in as Eddie blew out a plume of blue smoke from his quirly.

'We was a-wonderin' what all that shootin' was about?' He paused, fastening a gimlet eye on to the ashen-faced hardcase. Slowly Otero rose to his feet, followed by Dom Brewer. 'You know anything about that, John?'

Beswick laughed. It emerged as a nervous croak. A buzzard hovering above the trail joined in. But there was no cause for amusement. He rubbed his lacerated ear, knowing it was useless to deny the obvious. Best to tell the truth, doctored slightly in his favour.

'If'n yuh wanna know,' he began gingerly.

'We sure do, mister,' rasped Clayburn, rising to his feet and planting them squarely before the shuffling crop-ear. 'And it better be good.'

Beswick swallowed. 'Fact is, I recognized the marshal as being that skunk that slashed my ear. Nothing else mattered. I had to get my revenge on the bastard. You know how it is, Eddie.'

Clayburn remained close-mouthed. But his narrowed, frigid gaze said that he certainly did not know how it was. Nor did he want to. He'd heard enough.

'Your damn blasted obsession will have cost us dear,' he snarled out. 'The marshal might have bitten the dust, but there are others left. And they'll soon cotton to the fact it was all a set-up.'

'So what yuh gonna do about it?' Beswick knew he was not going to escape without a fight. He might be a more accurate shot but close up Eddie could easily outdraw him. He glanced at the other two. How would they react?

Only one way to find out.

Without waiting for the gang leader to make his decision, Beswick threw himself to one side, scrambling behind a nearby rock. Otero and Brewer dropped to their knees. Guns drawn, they triggered a couple of shots each before seeking cover of their own on the far side of the trail.

Eddie alone remained, unphased by the reckless abandon of his adversary. He backed off a few paces loosening the revolver in its holster.

'You ain't goin' no place, John.' The rancid snarl was biting. 'Raise your darned fool head and these guys'll blow it off. Best to come out now and have it out with me.'

'You know I can't match you for speed,' replied

Beswick from behind the rock. 'I'll take my chances here, thanks.'

Eddie quickly joined his loyal compadres. It was a stand-off. And time was passing. Something had to be done to bring the matter to a conclusion – in Eddie Clayburn's favour.

For five minutes neither faction spoke.

Then Eddie offered a compromise. 'Only one of us is going to walk away from here. You know that don't you, John?'

'What yuh suggestin'?' replied Beswick, his interest pricked.

'To make us equal in the gun totin' stakes,' Eddie declared, 'I'll lay my revolver on the ground. We spin a coin and when it hits the ground. . . .' There was no need to say more. 'What about it? You'll have the edge then. And just to show I ain't playin' tricks, here. . . .'

He threw out his gun which fell to the ground with a dull thud. Then slowly, and with careful deliberation, he emerged from cover. With arms raised, he stepped out into the open.

'And if I win, you order them other two varmints to let me go,' Beswick prompted warily. 'I ride away free as a bird. Agreed?'

'You heard the guy, fellas,' Eddie called out to his buddies. 'If John guns me down fair and square, he goes free.'

Otero and Slippery Dom glanced uncertainly at one another. What was Eddie playing at? Sure he was fast, but not that fast. Or was he?

Assured that he was not stepping into a trap, John Beswick joined Clayburn in the open, his right hand flexing close to the butt of his pistol. The two desperadoes faced each other no more than twelve feet apart.

Eddie studied his opponent with a practised eye. A nervous tick above his left temple betrayed Beswick's disquiet. He chewed his lower lip psyching himself for the inevitable finale.

Eddie's face remained flat, devoid of expression, inscrutable and innocent of guile. He reached into his vest pocket and extracted a silver dollar.

'Remember the bargain,' he stressed settling the coin on his thumbnail. 'Only go for your gun when it hits the ground.'

A curt nod from Beswick.

The coin spun skywards, slivers of light from a dying sun reflecting off the shiny metal. Over and over, to its zenith, then down, down down, until. . . .

Beswick grabbed for his pistol. He even managed to palm it before Eddie's bullet struck him in the chest. A second later the next bullet took Cropper John's good ear off. His hogleg slipped from nerveless fingers. The stricken outlaw tottered, his rapidly blurring gaze fixed on to the small nickel-plated .22 pocket revolver.

Eddie's main handgun still lay on the ground, untouched.

'Didn't think I was gonna let you go that easily, did you John?' sniggered the outlaw boss. With purposeful deliberation, he bent down and retrieved the Colt

.45, cocked it and shot his unlucky antagonist in the head.

Without a backward glance he moved across to his horse and swung lithely into the saddle.

'OK, boys,' he announced with breezy disregard for his deception. 'We got us a bank to rob, and another pesky burr to remove. The three of us should have no problems on that score. We can put a few more miles behind us afore sundown.'

FOURTEEN

LAST CHANCE SALOON

Early the following morning Sol and his two remaining posse members entered the outskirts of Tatum Bend. The town sat on a low terrace beside the dried-up trench of the Arroyo Del Macho, a tributary of the Pecos. A tiny isolated settlement, its sole purpose was to collect gold from prospectors working the foothills of the Capitans. In consequence the main building in town was the assay office.

Sol signalled a halt. The place looked deserted.

'Mighty peculiar,' he muttered. 'I'd have reckoned the place would have been buzzing by sun-up.'

'Could be they're all workin' their claims,' suggested Skip Logan.

'Or maybe havin' themselves a lie-in,' added Colorado Bob. 'After all, it is Saturday. We allus did when Buck Swaggert and me was pannin' the Animas around Silverton.'

Sol gave the suggestions a sceptical frown. He wasn't convinced.

Bob scratched his thinning patch of greasy hair. 'I seem to recall one dingdong back in '72 when—'

'Not now, eh Bob,' Sol murmured, interrupting the old-timer's reminiscences and nudging his mount forward. 'And keep your guns handy, boys,' he warned settling the sawn-off shotgun across his lap. 'Just in case.'

Rounding a curve in the main street, they came across the first human being. And he was not one to inspire confidence. Propped up against an upright supporting the veranda canopy, there was blood streaming down the guy's face from a head wound.

Sol leapt from the saddle and hurried across to the stricken man.

'What in thunder happened here, mister?' he shouted easing the injured man into a nearby chair. 'That cut needs attention, pronto.' He indicated for Logan to pass his water bottle. He splashed liquid on to his bandanna and wiped away the blood, revealing a wicked gash across the guy's forehead. 'Is there a sawbones in town?' he asked dabbing at the ragged laceration.

Griff Sumner, the assay agent, shook his head. 'Tatum Bend is too small. We do our own doctorin'.'

'And where is everybody?' enquired Logan handing Sol his own necker to help stanch the flow of blood.

The injured man breathed deep before answering.

'Too darned scared to come out after the robbery.' His head drooped. 'Three men rode in and came straight into the office. They shot my assistant.' He took another gulp of air as he nodded towards the open door of the office. 'I reckon he must be dead. The foolhardy critter went for his gun. Didn't stand a chance. All three of the varmints gunned him down.'

Sol turned to address his other posse member. 'You go see if he's still alive, Frank.'

So there were three, commented Sol to himself. 'What did they look like?'

'Meanest bunch I ever did see.' Sumner's whole body trembled as he recalled the brutal attack. 'They took the gold dust waiting for shipment and around a thousand bucks from the safe.'

'Can you describe them?' asked Sol, fearing the worst.

'The leader was a young punk with blond hair, no more'n twenty three. A cold hard-ass who the others referred to as Eddie. Can't recall their features. He hit me with the barrel of his gun afore I had time to say anything. Laid me out cold.'

The agent was dazed, and that cut needed stitching. But Sol didn't have any time to spare.

'When was this?' he pressed. Sol's voice expressed the urgency of his question. The punk kid had to be Eddie Clayburn.

'What time is it now?' asked the agent, accepting a drink of water.

'A quarter after ten,' Sol shot back, not meaning to be harsh, but itching to be on the move.

'Errrrm,' mused the injured man. 'Musta been two hours since.'

Two hours!

He would have to set a furious pace to catch them up. If the gang reached Tularosa first, there was no knowing what they would do when they found him absent. It didn't bear thinking on.

Sumner's eyes rolled skyward. The guy was all in. He was on the verge of losing consciousness. And with responsibility for three bodies of his own, Sol knew that he didn't have a hope of getting back to Tularosa in time to avert a disaster.

Unless. The glimmer of an idea formed in his racing mind. What if he left the boys here to look after these guys? They could then bring their own dead back to Tularosa in due course.

It was the only way.

At that moment Colorado Bob came staggering out of the assay office. His face was greener than a cactus in full bloom. Lurching to the side of the building he emptied his guts into the street.

'Dead, ugh?' muttered Sol. The comment needed no confirmation.

Bob had been a goldminer and mountain man, a real tough nut, before settling down to raise chickens on a plot of scrub land on the outskirts of Tularosa. It must have been one ugly sight to upset him like that.

'They drilled the poor sap then blasted him at

point-blank range with a shotgun,' groaned Bob holding his stomach. 'Ain't enough left for even his wife to recognize.'

Sol gave the old guy a look of sympathy, then told them what he had decided.

'I'm carrying on back to Tularosa alone. You fellas stay here and see what you can do, then follow me in.'

Sol didn't wait for any comments on his proposed action. His mind was fully made up and nothing would sway him from his endeavour. He hurried over to his horse and vaulted into the saddle. Before departing, however, he did consider that a brief explanation was required.

'This is the gang that robbed our bank and shot down Russ Bradley and Doc Farthing. Now they're after me. And if I ain't available, it'll be my family what gets it.'

Then he slapped leather and pounded off up the street, heading west.

Eddie Clayburn stopped on the outskirts of Tularosa. How many times had he been forced to return to this hick town? It was like a thorn in his side. Well, this was gonna be the last. No way was he leaving without having avenged the slaying of his brother once and for all.

The gang had been reduced in numbers, but there was no reason why they couldn't pull this off. It had been a stroke of luck happening on that assay office in Tatum Bend. Maybe they didn't need to hit

144

the bank. Just go in, kill the store clerk and light out for pastures new. His hands caressed the shotgun acquired from Cropper John.

That posse would likely be hot on their trail. Even if they hadn't become suspicious following Beswick's hotheaded brainstorming, they would have surely figured some underhand skulduggery was afoot following the skunk's execution. Perhaps he should have used a knife. His shoulders lifted in a careless shrug. Too late for regrets now.

All these speculations filtered through his brain as he studied the main street. He could have found the gunstore blindfolded. And just as well. He felt certain they were a good four hours ahead of the posse having convinced himself that they would decide to return to Tularosa. Still, there was plenty of time for what he had in mind. No sense pushing your luck. Best get it over with quick and disappear before any prying busybodies blew the whistle.

Then again, with the town wide open, why not hit the bank?

'Lucky we arrived near to closing time,' Eddie said through the side of his mouth. He was feeling confident. 'Gives us time to go in and have the place to ourselves.'

A gentle squeeze of the knees and his sorrel mare edged forward down the left side of the street. Even with the sun still bathing the town in a rosy glow, he was positive that nobody would recognize them.

A block down from the gun store, he drew to a halt.

'You stay here,' he ordered Slippery Dom brusquely. 'Keep Otero and me covered while I do what has to be done. It shouldn't take more'n a single shot. Any more gunplay and you come a-runnin'. Savvy?'

'Sure thing, boss,' grunted the thin weasel. 'You can count on me.'

After tying off their mounts, the blond-haired kid and his stocky subordinate casually strolled across the street. Eddie peered in through the window of the gun shop. No customers. With a brisk nod of satisfaction he went in and immediately switched the 'open' sign around to 'closed'.

A young kid of around nine years of age was reading a comic behind the counter. He hadn't noticed Clayburn's quick manoeuvre.

'Your pa in, boy?' grunted the gunman.

The boy shook his head.

Eddie glowered back. 'Where is he? We got urgent business with him.'

'Pa's gone off with the posse,' explained an unsuspecting Billy Henshaw. 'There was a payroll robbery over at Capitan Pass. It was that ornery bunch of snakes, the Clayburn Gang what done it.'

Eddie bristled, his fists clenched. So much for Beswick's assertion that only single men are chosen for a posse. Otero sensed the anger building. He stepped forward.

'Where's yer ma?'

Billy slung a thumb to his left. 'Down the street someplace.'

146

Eddie moved away, ostensibly to study the guns on display. But his mind was spinning furiously. So Henshaw had been with the posse all along. If only he'd recognized the skunk, he could have finished him off at the pass.

Still, all was not lost. He had the kid. They could hold him as a hostage. An upstanding citizen like Henshaw would not risk his son's life. Exchange one for another. It had to be the answer.

Without further ado, Eddie leant across and grabbed Billy by his shirt, yanking him clean over the counter. The boy was taken completely by surprise. But he soon recovered and began squirming about like a greasy slab of fatback trying to escape the assailant's firm grip.

'You leave me be!' he yelled. 'What d'yuh want?'

A solid punch to the boy's jaw soon put a stop to any further resistance. Blood spilled from a cut lip. Billy was stunned but still retained the nous to understand the horror that these must be the varmints who were after killing his pa.

'You'll never get him now,' he laughed. 'And when he comes back, you rats will be the ones eatin' dirt.' The jibe drew forth another painful backhander that sent him spinning across the room.

Frustration was bubbling over as Eddie moved across, intending to vent his spleen on the helpless youth with a brutal kick in the ribs. But at that moment the door opened.

Eddie spun round. His mouth dropped. He'd forgotten to lock up. And there, silhouetted in the late afternoon sun was the comely shape of a women. It took less than a second for Maddy Henshaw to take in the grim situation that met her distraught gaze.

She flew across the room, sharp nails tearing at the gunman's face. Twin tracks of red appeared on Eddie's right cheek. He uttered a yowl of pain, flinging the she-tiger off. His hand instinctively dropped to the gun on his hip. An enraged snarl spat from pursed lips.

Otero saw what was about to happen. He reached out and clamped his leader's gunhand in a grip of steel.

'We don't kill women or kids,' he rasped in a flat tone that brooked no denial. 'That was Rafe's ruling and it's mine as well.' He fixed a baleful eye on the young hothead. It was Eddie who lowered his gaze first.

'OK,' he muttered, stalking away. 'But get these bastards trussed up tighter than a Thanksgiving turkey.'

Mumbling under his breath he proceeded to exchange his own well-used firearm for the latest Colt .45. He felt sure that it would soon be put to the test on a human target.

Then they settled down to await the arrival of their prey. All thoughts of robbing the bank had been abandoned. This current change to their circumstances had effectivly scuppered all that. All he wanted now was to finish the job he had originally planned and light out of this blamed territory for good.

Tularosa had become an irritating pain that was gnawing at his vitals, a millstone around his neck. A more rational being would have cut his losses and lit out there and then. But Eddie Clayburn was anything but prudent. Indeed he was proving to be a veritable psychopath.

Otero knew that he also should have quit the gang while he had the chance. A gimlet glare drilled in to the back of his old buddy's unhinged brother. It was only his loyalty to Rafe that had prevented him flying the coop. Now he was in this to the end. However that might turn out.

FIFTEEN

TWO LIVES
FOR ONE

Sol Henshaw arrived back in Tularosa an hour later.
He had ridden non-stop from Tatum Bend. His
mount was lathered and on the verge of collapse.

'What are you doing back here?' enquired Hyram
Swinburn, puffing his chest out pompously. 'The
posse too much to cope with?'

Sol ignored the slight to his manhood.

'The marshal's been shot dead and I have every
reason to believe the Clayburns are heading back this
way,' he rasped with undisguised disdain. 'Now get
everyone off the street.'

The bank manager's face darkened. His hackles
rose. Nobody ordered Hyram Swinburn around. He
tried to exert his authority. But it was a weak-kneed
effort. The determined glint in the ex-pugilist's fixed

gaze, his stoic bearing, vigorously cowed any further protest.

'So what you waiting for?' snapped Sol impatiently.

The banker hurried off without another word.

Sol tied up two blocks down from his store and approached the gun shop warily.

Over on the far side, Brewer saw the killer of his esteemed leader acting with marked care and hesitancy. He ducked round the end of a saddler's, keeping out of sight as he nervously tried to fathom the guy's intentions.

Gun palmed, Brewer was unsettled. He was unused to making decisions. Should he cut the fella down before he could barge into the store? Or wait and see what happened?

The choice was effectively made for him as Sol decided to enter the store from the rear. He had no idea whether the gang had arrived in Tularosa, although all his instincts screamed out that they must have. So were they inside holding his family hostage? Or had they removed them to a safer unknown location?

There was only one way to find out.

Round the back of his store, Sol peered through the window into a stockroom. But he could see nothing. He removed his own key from a pocket and made to enter by the rear door. Before he could do so a shadow cast by the dipping afternoon sun played across his right shoulder.

It saved him from being pole-axed by Dom Brewer's pistol butt. Ducking beneath the swingeing attempt to lay him out, Sol felt the draught as the gun whipped past his exposed head. With Brewer thrown off balance Sol grabbed his gun arm and wrestled the outlaw to the ground.

After a couple of slams against the side of the building Brewer was forced to relinquish his weapon. Sol hauled the guy to his feet and rammed a bunched fist into his face. Brewer grunted, his nose erupting in a stream of blood as he staggered back. But the skinny guy was no pushover. Well versed in the brutal art of street fighting, he shrugged off the assault and drew a knife from inside his jacket.

An evil grin cracked open the outlaw's leaden features. Slowly the two adversaries circled one another warily. In the old days, Solomon King would have displayed extra caution with a wiry and dangerous opponent like Brewer. But he was in a hurry. It was now clear that Clayburn was in the store and holding his family hostage.

He rushed the weasel, trying to get a grip on his knife hand. Slippery Dom lived up to his nickname by stepping aside and angling an upward slice at Sol's face. The attacker just managed to evade the full force of the swipe that would have carved his face open to the bone had it connected. It did, however, rip through his shirt front. He cried out in pain as the sharp blade drew blood. Not serious but enough to urge caution and a change of tactics.

He backed away from the slippery dude. A plan had formed in his mind. Brewer now sensed that he had the advantage and pressed forward his attack.

152

Jabbing and feinting, a series of incomprehensible mumbles and grunts heralded the charge that was imminent. The warped grin grew ever wider.

Letting his arms fall as if accepting the inevitable, Sol allowed his opponent to think he was finished. Brewer perceived victory as he surged forward, only to find a barrel that had been standing close by over-turned and rolled into his path.

The outlaw stumbled over it, dropping his knife and allowing Sol to step in close. A couple of solid haymakers delivered to the side of the head dis-patched the outlaw into the land of oblivion. Sol reached for a lariat hanging on a wall hook, tethered the guy and dragged him inside the stockroom.

Not a word had been spoken during the entire contest.

But the noisy fracas had been heard by those inside the store. Eddie correctly assumed that his back-up had tangled with their quarry. But had he succeeded in neutralizing the gun merchant? Clayburn waited, his new Colt jammed into the ear of Maddy Henshaw.

Otero took cover behind the counter.

Silence descended as they counted the seconds. If Brewer had managed to take the critter out, he would have appeared by now.

'You hear me, Henshaw?' hollered the outlaw. 'I got your wife and kid all trussed up in here. One false move and they're dogmeat. You got one way for them to come outa this unscathed. And I guess you know what that is.'

'I hear you, Clayburn,' came back the subdued response. 'You better not have harmed them, otherwise—'

'Don't worry,' the outlaw cut Sol's words short. 'Just a little mussed up, is all. What did you do with that half-witted knucklehead, Dom Brewer?'

'He's taking a nap,' replied Sol, trying to inject some measure of belligerence into the remark. 'Things got a mite hot for the slippery cuss.'

'Well, he can stay there.' Clayburn snorted. 'The lunkhead was supposed to warn us when you arrived, not get hisself in a mess.'

'You ain't leavin' him, are you Eddie?' asked Otero.

'Why not?' Clayburn snapped back. 'Because of him, we could have been trapped, up the creek for darned sure. Now we've got the chance to get out and start up afresh with a solid grubstake.'

'So what happens now?' shouted Sol from the back room.

'All you have to do now, mister, is follow me out of town so that we ain't disturbed. Then we can make the swap. Your life for theirs. Fair exchange I'd say.' Eddie couldn't resist a hearty guffaw. 'You ready to make the ultimate sacrifice, big man?' There was no reply, which Eddie took as an affirmative. 'So this is how we play it,' he said.

Ten minutes later Eddie Clayburn and Otero had saddled up and were leading their two gagged and bound captives out of town, both riding on Brewer's

154

horse. They took a back trail to avoid any unwelcome attention.

Sol had been given firm instructions to follow alone after another ten minutes. They would meet up at Benson's Yard, two miles to the west, where the exchange would be made.

The corral had been abandoned two years before after the owner, Frank Benson, had been found with an Apache arrow in his back. The wrangler had figured to escape having to pay rent to the council by establishing his horse-trading business outside the town limits. Unbeknowing, the poor sap had left himself wide open to Indian raids on his stock and paid for it with his life.

Sol Henshaw's life was also now on the line.

'If'n I see anybody followin' you, it's curtains for these two. And the dame gets it first,' Clayburn had informed him, leaving Sol fully convinced that he would carry out the threat.

Sol had no intentions of seeking any help.

Indeed he was under no illusions that any would be offered. Swinburn would have passed the word. Like as not the townsfolk would all be cowering under their beds waiting for the action to start and hoping he would get drilled. Then they could all settle down once again to their mundane existence. The notion brought a spurt of bile to his throat. He spat the rancid taste into the dust.

When he arrived at the corral his wife and son were securely tied to the fencing. Even though they were unable to speak, their terrible anguish was etched deeply across drawn faces. They were helpless witnesses in this bizarre situation.

Like a slavering dog, Clayburn was eagerly awaiting his victim. Otero looked uncomfortable, his boot toeing the dirt.

'Step down and walk slowly to the middle of the corral,' Clayburn growled. 'Then say *adios* to your kin.' With slow deliberation he levered a round into the barrel of the Winchester and raised the rifle to his shoulder.

For Sol it was a walk from which there could be no return. But he kept his head held high, even managing a smile for his family. My life for yours. The words were silently mouthed. The pain and misery for all three was excruciating. Each step, dragging in the dust, brought him nearer to the end. His legs felt like jelly. But he endeavoured to maintain a stoic resolve, determined not to display any sign of weakness to the odious executioner.

Clayburn's finger tightened on the trigger.

That was when Otero decided he couldn't take any more.

'This ain't right, Eddie,' he blurted out. 'Rafe would never have sunk this low. Sure he was a thief and a killer. But he had standards that you've thrown out the window.'

With surprising speed for such a stocky jasper, he ran across and grabbed a hold of the rifle. The two outlaws wrestled, each struggling for supremacy. Caught totally off guard by the sudden challenge of his treacherous confederate, Clayburn backed off.

'What in thunderation are you playin' at?' he ejaculated, trying to fend off the sudden attack from behind. 'You gone crazy, Otero, you sonofabitch?'

Otero knew that he was the loser however this confrontation ended. But he couldn't just stand by and let Eddie play God.

Sol had been caught equally unawares. Out of the blue, he had been handed a lifeline. And he intended making full use of it. Without further delay, he dashed across the intervening stretch of open ground.

The two outlaws continued their fight over possession of the rifle. Otero was a wily critter and caught the kid a numbing blow to the side of the head. But Clayburn's youth and superior strength was too much for the ageing outlaw. He soon got the upper hand, pushing Otero away. Then, with a stunning side-swipe, the rifle butt knocked him senseless.

'I'll deal with you after I've finished this turkey off,' he snarled turning back to face the charging figure now hurtling towards him.

Sol was still twenty feet away when the rifle was pointed his way for the second time. Had his chance for survival been torn from his grasp?

Suddenly the quiet of late afternoon was shattered by a thunderous roar. And not from Eddie Clayburn's rifle. The outlaw was struck by a volley of bullets that ripped into his body. Pitching and cavorting, he spun round like a dancing marionette eventually tumbling to the ground in a heap of blood-soaked rags.

Sol stopped his forward lunge, staring open-mouthed at the grotesque tableau that his eyes struggled to comprehend. Time stood still in Benson's Yard. For what seemed a lifetime, he was mesmerized, frozen to the spot.

Then, slowly, the truth dawned. He was alive, and so were his wife and son.

Hurrying across, he freed them. All three clung together, tears of joy and relief soaking their clothes. It was a movement behind that eventually caused Sol to open his eyes. For a brief second he figured it was all a nightmare. He was dead and this was all a sham.

Then a voice he recognized spoke up. 'You OK, Sol?'

It was Hyram Swinburn. He was accompanied by a dozen more Tularosa citizens. They were all looking decidedly sheepish, ashamed even.

'We're real sorry at the way you've been treated over this last few weeks,' Swinburn said rubbing his hands nervously. 'I feel downright mortified that I wanted you to leave Tularosa when you needed the town's full backing. It's taken this to bring us all to our senses.'

Tucker Welch, the blacksmith, chimed in to save the mayor further embarrassment. 'We followed you out here and hid behind the old barn,' he explained. 'Them cottonwoods helped keep us out of sight. It's lucky that the other critter butted in, else we would have been too late.'

They all looked across to where Otero was struggling to his feet.

Two of the rescuers hustled across and pinioned him. His gun was removed and without too much care, he was dragged across to face his captors.

The outlaw had nothing to say. Whatever they decided to hand out, he knew was well and truly deserved. One angry townsman cuffed him around the head.

'What we gonna do with this turkey?' enquired the blacksmith.

'I say we string him up here and now,' offered another irate jigger. 'Send a message out that Tularosa don't welcome outlaws and desperadoes.'

A general chorus of agreement greeted this suggestion.

But Sol firmly vetoed the terminal solution. He held up a hand for silence.

'This guy saved my bacon,' he told the townsmen firmly. 'He didn't have to. Could have gone along with Clayburn and rode away with a heap of dough in their saddle-bags. But he chose to raise a challenge. I for one am more'n grateful to the guy.'

'So what you suggesting then, Sol?' asked Swinburn.

'There's been enough killing.' He cast a penetrating eye across the gathering. 'I say we let him go . . . without the loot, of course.' Again he peered around the group, silently urging them to show mercy.

The proposal received some murmurs of disapprobation, but there were nods of approval.

And so it was agreed.

Otero mounted up. 'Much obliged, mister.' The

outlaw's gratitude came from the heart.

As he turned to leave, Sol grasped the bridle of his horse. In a low voice laced with menace he offered a stark warning. 'But if you ever come back this way again, I won't be so accommodating. Get my drift?'

A shiver fluttered down the outlaw's spine as he nodded his understanding. Anxious he get away, he then spurred off at a reckless gallop.

Sol slung his arms around the shoulders of the two people he most valued, then walked away from the fateful corral followed by his rescuers.